Also by Mercedes Ron

Culpables
My Fault
Your Fault
Our Fault

Tell Me
Tell Me Softly
Tell Me in Secret
Tell Me with Kisses

Tell Me in Secret

MERCEDES RON

Bloom books

Published by Bloom Books, an imprint of Sourcebooks
1935 Brookdale RD, Naperville, IL 60563-2773
(630) 961-3900
sourcebooks.com

Originally self-published in 2020 by Mercedes Ron.

Cataloging-in-Publication data is on file with the Library of Congress.

Printed and bound in the United States of America.
LSC 10 9 8 7 6 5 4 3 2 1

To all the people who ever
thought they weren't good enough.
You are!

Content Warning

This book contains references to sexual assault, cyberbullying, harassment, and physical assault.

PROLOGUE

Kami

THERE WE WERE, GETTING INTO TROUBLE AGAIN. BUT THIS TIME, it was the older one's fault. The one who was supposed to be more responsible.

He'd dragged us out here in the middle of the night, and the first thing he'd done was take a lighter, a piece of metal, and a first aid kit out of his backpack. It didn't bode well, but that was just how Thiago Di Bianco was. And we always did what he said. He was older, and that was his right. He got to be the boss; it was as simple as that.

I had problems sticking to the rules sometimes though, especially when they came from a guy who had no problem pulling my hair or making me cry. But I had to admit I always felt safe with him, no matter how dangerous our adventures were. He was almost a father figure, and he always reassured us that we weren't screwing things up.

But the way he treated me had changed since we'd gone on our candy raid and I'd given him a kiss. He'd stopped pulling my braids, but he'd turned bossier, and it seemed like he was always trying to get my attention.

"What are you gonna do with that?" I asked, looking at the lighter.

Thiago's ideas were getting riskier and riskier, and it took courage to keep up with him. I was open to adventure, but I had my limits. Or maybe it was the age difference—I mean, I was only ten and a half.

"Nothing you can't handle," he replied, getting up and walking over to the lookout, where he'd left his backpack.

I caught Taylor's eye; he was watching the scene nervously.

We were in our tree house; we sometimes called it *the fort.* Thiago had put tons of effort into it, but it still looked like it could fall apart at any second. This was the first time Taylor had been up there, and you could tell he was impressed.

He took my hand and said, "Don't be afraid, Kami. I'm here with you."

I smiled just as Thiago brought his own hand down on top of ours. "You don't even know what we're doing yet," he said, sitting down. He was still clutching the lighter, and he showed us the piece of metal wire he'd been trying to hide earlier. At one end, it was bent into a triangle. "Do you know what this is?" he asked. And since neither of us answered, he responded, "It's proof of our friendship."

"How is that piece of metal supposed to be proof of our friendship?" I asked, looking at it and the lighter and wondering what on earth he was up to.

Thiago stared me down and said, "There's nothing more lasting than a tattoo, is there?" And he flicked the little wheel on the lighter, drawing a spark. "And since we're going to be friends forever, what's the best way to show it?"

Starting to look worried, Taylor asked, "What are you saying, Thiago?"

But his brother didn't answer.

He held the triangle over the flame, long enough for it to glow orange, and when he was sure I was watching him, he pressed the burning metal into his wrist, pursing his lips and closing his eyes as it seared his flesh.

"Thiago, stop!" I shouted, but he didn't listen. He managed to take it for a few more seconds, then he pulled the brand away. Taylor and I bent over to see the result. It was bright red and a little wrinkly.

"Are you crazy?" I asked. I couldn't believe what he'd just done.

"Did it hurt?" Taylor asked, looking on in shock.

"Not too bad..." Thiago responded, turning his wrist back and forth. The triangle was now a part of him, clear as day, and would be forever. "So who's next?"

Eyes wide, Taylor and I stared at each other, both terrified.

"There's no way you're burning that into my hand!" Taylor shouted.

"It's your wrist, not your hand, dummy," Thiago corrected him. He didn't seem to care what his brother thought—his eyes were on me. "What do you say, princess? You want to get a real tattoo, or are you a scaredy-cat like Tay here?" he asked, not caring how much his words might sting his brother.

"Don't call me *princess*," I said. I took a deep breath, got to my knees, and rolled up the sleeve of my sweatshirt. "Do it," I told him, not even blinking.

I can still remember how proud he looked.

How proud he was and how painful that stupid idea ended up being.

CHAPTER ONE

Kami

IT HAD BEEN TWO WEEKS SINCE THE COLD IN CARSVILLE HAD settled in, wiping out any last traces of summer, any warm sunlight, leaving us with torrential rains, tornado warnings, and few reasons to go out and enjoy ourselves. But then I didn't have money to do anything anyway. Dad's situation was only getting worse. I would've done anything to spend an evening in town, dropping by Mill's and having a strawberry shake or a coffee and a chocolate muffin…but I could forget that. I didn't even have a car anymore.

At least I could still look out my window. But even that was a double-edged sword. Because I couldn't stop following the movements of the girl who had been there for half an hour, passing Thiago his tools and showing off her long legs in a miniskirt.

It was fifty-two degrees out. Wasn't she cold?

And where had this girl come from? How had he met her?

She was pretty, I couldn't deny that. Her hair was long and dark, her eyes blue, I was pretty sure. She was standing far away, but there had been a second when she'd turned, and in that same second the one ray of sunlight we'd seen that day had broken through the clouds, reflecting the light in her eyes. Damn it. She was beautiful. Tall, thin, perfect.

This naturally made me think of my own appearance. Five-five, shoulder-length blond hair starting to fade to a dusty brown since I hadn't seen the beach in months... I felt like a damn frog compared to her.

Those hands... Hands now wrapped around the girl's waist, but two weeks ago those hands had been all mine, in Thiago's car in the middle of a storm. If I closed my eyes and remembered it, my heart started racing, my body got hot, and my thighs squeezed together involuntarily. My mind flashed back to that day as I imagined what would have happened if we'd done more than kiss; what it would have felt like to have his hands on my skin, my breasts, his fingers giving me pleasure, his eyes on mine, our bodies joined together...

Someone knocked on my door and killed the fantasy.

"Kamila, your father and I want to talk to you," my mother said, peeking in. "Come down to the living room please."

She closed the door, and I heard her walk downstairs. I looked out the window; there was Thiago kissing her...

Something ached inside me. I don't know what it was. My heart was bleeding with lovesickness or desire or I don't know what. I was hurting. Bad.

I closed my curtains and stood.

What did my parents want now?

For weeks, I'd been shut up in my room, blasting music so I wouldn't have to hear them shouting, trying to flee far away in my mind.

Taylor had tried to get me out a few times. He had driven me to Stony Creek to catch a movie or just sit at Starbucks and chat for a few hours. We were getting closer and closer by the day, and I felt an almost addictive need for his company, his kisses, the way he cared for me and made me laugh.

I don't know how he did it, but every time we were together, he just made our problems disappear. I even forgot about Thiago when I was with him. It was like nothing existed except for Taylor and Kami, best friends forever...or a little more than that.

And yet, when he wasn't with me, I couldn't help but feel split in two. My heart wanted one guy, but I was hungry for another one...and that made me feel like the worst person in the world.

I went downstairs and into the living room. My mom was sitting on the couch facing the fireplace, which we'd started to use in the last two weeks. It was crazy that, just like that, the good weather was over and there was a fall chill in the air.

My brother, Cameron, was splayed out on the other sofa, absorbed in his Nintendo Switch, the sound of *Super Mario Party* filling the room. He had been standoffish as hell the past few days. He didn't want anyone to hug him, he didn't want to play in the yard, he just spent all his time there in front of the TV, playing video games, or watching cartoons. I could hardly remember the little six-year-old tadpole who used to be able to turn my mood around in an instant no matter how upset I was.

"So what's up?" I asked my parents, settling down next to Cameron.

Dad had been stacking logs beside the fireplace. He stood up straight, put the tongs aside, and looked at us and then at Mom, who announced, "Kids, your father and I are getting a divorce."

My mind froze at the same time Cam hit mute on the Nintendo and the entire room went silent.

"What?" I asked once I'd recovered somewhat from the blow.

I got it: My parents fought. My mom was unbearable. But they loved each other, didn't they? They'd even gotten over her having an affair. Dad was someone who knew how to forgive, or so I thought...

"We've been talking it over, and we don't think it's healthy for you two to live in an environment where two people are fighting all the time," Dad said.

"*You* never fight," I reminded him. "It's always her."

Fear, rage, and impotence were boiling up inside me, and I felt like a pressure cooker about to explode.

"Kamila!" Mom shouted indignantly. "This isn't some kind of joke, and you don't get to have a say! Sometimes, love runs out and—"

"Oh, please!" I cut her off, standing up. "Don't come at me with this *love* bullshit. It has nothing to do with love running out. It's the money!"

I tried to see Dad's reaction, but he looked down at the floor. Christ. I could tell Dad didn't want this.

"How dare you…"

"How dare I?" I screamed back. I was beside myself. "He has one setback, and you leave him in the lurch! Things get a little complicated, and you can't go to the spa, you can't blow money every day at the mall, Dad merely *suggests* you might need to get a cheaper car, and bang! You want a divorce."

"That's enough, Kamila," Dad said.

"I don't know what makes you think you can talk to me like that, you spoiled little brat," Mom hissed.

I roared back at her incredulously, "*Spoiled*! I'm the one who's spoiled?"

My mother's mouth opened to respond, but then Dad's fist struck the coffee table, and we all fell silent.

"That's enough!" he shouted. "This isn't up for debate. We've made our decision, Kamila, we're getting a divorce, and we know perfectly well that you don't like it. But we need to talk about how things are going to proceed and—"

"I'm going with you," I told him without hesitation. "I'm not living with her. And I'm sure as hell not leaving you alone, Dad."

"No. You're staying with your mother."

I looked over at Cam, who was frozen and listening attentively.

"We want to do this in the most civilized way possible. And right now, I'm not even sure where I'm going to be living. There's not much work for financial advisers in Carsville, so I'll have to go somewhere else. I'm trying to stay as close to home as possible, but there are no guarantees. You and your brother are halfway through the school year, and you don't need the disruption, especially now, when you'll have to start applying for college. You need stability, and that means staying here at your home with your mother is the best thing."

"What?" My eyes were filling with tears. "Dad, I... I don't want you to go." I felt like a little girl, completely unequipped to deal with my emotions.

"I'll try to come see you guys on the weekends..."

"Maybe, Roger. Don't get ahead of yourself. There's a lot that's still up in the air. You shouldn't go making promises to the girl you can't keep."

I looked at her with hatred. "Don't call me *girl*. And don't come at me with any bullshit about promises and whatever. He's my father, he loves me, he *will* come see me, won't you, Dad?"

"No one said you won't see him," my mother said with irritation. "But as long as you're in this house, I'm your guardian, I make the rules, and visitation is something your father and I need to work out together."

I laughed bitterly. "I'm eighteen, Mom. Try me with your rules and see if I don't just move out."

"Kamila..." my father rebuked me.

"Don't you start in too," I told him. "If I want, I'll move in with you right now. There's not a damn thing she can do about it legally."

I stood up, walked around the coffee table, and stomped upstairs.

I couldn't believe it.

Just when I thought my mother couldn't fall any lower.

I cried, hugging my pillow, scared of the uncertainty I was facing. How could she leave him? She was the one who had been unfaithful. She was the one who had lied to all of us. Now she had split two families apart. It was her fault Taylor and Thiago's sister was dead. It was her fault Katia Di Bianco had lost the thing she loved most...

Mom was the one who should leave. This house was my father's. *She* had never worked a day in her life. She was nothing more than a kept woman. She'd grown up in a wealthy family, and her biggest aspiration in life had been to find a husband who would pay for all her trips to spas, spiritual retreats, and discounted Chanel bags.

She was pathetic.

I cried myself to sleep and opened my eyes a few hours later. It was nighttime, and the wind was bellowing against my windows.

I sat up on my pillows and heard a knock at the door. I didn't answer, but it cracked open, and in peeked the person I loved most in this house.

"Kami," Cameron said, walking over now. "What's divorce?"

I closed my eyes and hugged him.

The next day, my father took us to school, dropping me off first near the high school entrance and then pulling down farther to the elementary school lot. The two schools were joined by a long hallway decorated with art made by all different classes. Now that I no longer had a car, either my parents drove me or I took my bike. It was harder on Cam than me—he didn't start until later. But, well... When I used to take him, he'd had to wait in the schoolyard, playing video games.

I crossed the parking lot and wedged my way through the packed halls. I no longer wanted to stay outside with my friends, who stood around laughing, gossiping, and sneaking cigarettes— acting like they were cooler than everyone else. Plus, I still hadn't talked to Kate, and the rest of my friends seemed to want to follow her everywhere she went.

At my locker, I took out the books I'd need for my next class. It was almost November, and that meant midterms were around the corner. We had projects to do, papers to write, presentations to give, and all that without counting the extracurricular activities we'd need to keep up with if we wanted to get into a good school.

And now it wasn't just a matter of getting into Yale—I'd need a scholarship. That had changed everything. There'd be no slacking off. My future was at stake, my independence...everything, basically.

"Hey, precious," a voice whispered from behind me.

I smiled and turned around, and there he was, leaning on the lockers.

"Hey," I said, feeling that warmth I needed more than ever.

"I told you I could bring you guys in today," Taylor said, tucking a strand of hair behind my ear.

"Dad insisted. I should have told you, but it slipped my mind."

"No worries." His blue eyes traveled over my face as his fingers gently brushed my cheeks. "Have you been crying?"

"No," I replied automatically.

"Kami..."

I turned, closed my locker, and walked away, saying, "See you in biology." Why hadn't I told him about my parents? One thing I did know was that I didn't want anyone feeling sorry for me. I didn't want anybody giving me pitiful looks or asking me if I was

OK. I wanted what was happening at home to stay a secret as long as possible.

"Hey, Kami, hold up!" Ellie shouted from the other end of the hall. I waited for her to come over. "How was your weekend?" she asked. She looked uncomfortable. I didn't blame her. I'd kept my distance from everybody except Taylor for the last two weeks.

"It could have been better," I responded, walking to Mr. Gómez's class.

"You heard about the party Friday, right?" she asked, trying to ignore my somber tone. "Since Halloween's on a weekday, Aaron said we could throw a party at his place on Friday."

Great, I thought. *Another party at Aaron Martin's house.*

Just the thought of it gave me a headache, but I did love Halloween. I loved getting dressed up and decorating my house, and I loved eating candy. I'd stick to the basics this year and take my brother out trick-or-treating; I could throw on a sheet with two holes in it for eyes. I could already imagine Taylor laughing as he saw me taking my brother around our neighborhood.

"You *will* come, won't you?" Ellie asked.

"I don't know, Ellie," I said, biting my lip as I walked into class. I sat in the first row, and she took the desk beside mine.

"Come on," she responded, disappointed. "You've looked like a zombie for weeks now, walking up and down the halls with that sad face, not saying a word to anyone. What's up with you? You can tell me. We're supposed to be best friends."

And we were. Out of all my friends, Ellie was the one I trusted most, the one I loved most, the one who was most like me. But lately I'd felt like a fish out of water.

"Kate even wants you to come," she blurted out at last. Like I cared. "She said she was hoping we'd all dress up in matching costumes, like you did back in elementary school."

Ellie was the only one who hadn't gone to grade school with us. She'd come from the big city, from New York, and she was open-minded. That's why we got along so well. She didn't have stupid prejudices like everyone else.

"If I do go, I'm going to dress how I want, not how Kate says I have to."

Ellie's face lit up. "So that means you'll come, right?"

When I saw her brown eyes light up like that, I knew I couldn't resist.

"If I have to…"

She gave me a hug as the teacher walked in and said, "All right, everyone, take out a pen and paper. We're having a pop quiz on matrices."

Ellie and I looked at each other in horror.

Karma, why do you hate me so much?

I struggled through the quiz. It's not that I hadn't been studying, it's just that I couldn't retain anything. With all the distractions in my head, I couldn't concentrate. My eyes would scan the letters and numbers, but my mind was too full of my own problems. Between my parents, my so-called friends turning their backs on me, and Taylor and Thiago…I just hoped I could get a decent grade, I couldn't allow myself to simply pass the test.

On my way out of class, I felt my phone vibrate in the back pocket of my jeans. I looked at the screen and rejected the call. It was my mother. No way I was talking to her. If I had my way, I wouldn't even speak to her for the rest of the year. She called back. I ignored her again.

"Who is it?" Ellie asked. She had been walking beside me on our way to the science lab.

"My mom."

She made a horrified face, and we both laughed. At that moment, the principal's voice came over the loudspeaker.

Kamila Hamilton, please come immediately to the principal's office.

Everyone in the hallway turned to look at me.

"What did you do?" Ellie asked.

"Nothing!"

I felt a twinge of fear. It must have something to do with those unanswered calls from Mom. What if something had happened to my parents or to my grandparents? Or worse?

"I'll see you later," I said, turning around.

Five minutes later, I was standing outside Principal Harrison's office. He was waiting for me.

"Good morning, Kamila," he said, waving me in and telling me to take a seat.

"What did I do this time?" I asked nervously.

He sat down at his desk and sighed.

"You? Nothing. Which is a welcome change," he responded calmly. "It's about Cameron…" Before he could go on, someone knocked at the door.

"Come in," Mr. Harrison said, and I looked back to see who it was. As the door opened, I found myself face-to-face with the source of all my nightly fantasies. My stomach tightened as our gazes met. He looked away before I could get lost in his emerald green eyes.

"Ah, Mr. Di Bianco," Harrison said. "I was just about to tell Miss Hamilton why I called her into the office."

"Good morning, sir. I decided to come here and talk with Kamila directly." Despite the circumstances, my name coming from his lips gave me a thrill.

He was so handsome. His dirty-blond hair was combed back and he had a five-o'clock shadow. He was tall, imposing. How did he do it? Why did he have to be so goddamn attractive?

"What happened to Cameron? Is he OK?" I asked, remembering all at once what the principal had been saying before Thiago walked in.

"He got in another fight," Harrison said, his expression serious. Thiago walked over and stood next to the principal.

"I will say, sir, I don't think Cameron is the one who started it. I've kept an eye on him lately, and these last two weeks he seems to be incredibly lonely. He doesn't play with the other kids, he sits by himself at recess, he seems completely absorbed in his Nintendo. I didn't want to tell you what was going on until I was certain, but I think some of Cameron's classmates are bullying him."

I felt something shatter inside me. "What?" I asked, voice trembling.

"Are you sure, Mr. Di Bianco? Because at this school, we have a zero-tolerance policy when it comes to bullying. If you know of someone who—"

"It's George Walker, sir," Thiago said, looking over at me. "He's the ringleader, and from what I can tell, the kids all do whatever he says."

"Danny's brother?" I asked. I couldn't believe what I was hearing.

"That's a serious accusation, Mr. Di Bianco. Do you have any evidence?"

Now things were starting to make sense. "My brother's been coming home for weeks with his face a wreck from fighting," I said.

"Sir, I only took over PE classes a few weeks ago, but it's been long enough to realize something isn't right."

It was true. Two weeks ago, the PE teacher for the little kids had quit for personal reasons, and since then Thiago had taken over. My brother had been going on constantly about his new teacher, who was also his neighbor, and how much they were learning and how fun PE had become. My brother had been begging my dad for a basketball and a hoop so he could follow in the footsteps of his new idol: Thiago.

"What happened to him?" I asked, livid.

"I've seen people picking on Cam, insulting him, even hitting him. We teachers have been trying to intervene, but Cam keeps saying they're just playing."

"What makes you so sure that they aren't?" the principal asked.

I shot him a cold stare. I couldn't believe he'd ask such a thing—my little brother was the sweetest kid around; he wouldn't hurt a fly.

Thiago answered him in a chilling voice: "Locking a child in a bathroom stall all morning doesn't sound to me like a game anyone would go along with, Mr. Harrison."

The principal coughed, nodded, and arranged some papers on his desk.

I understood now. George Walker, just like his brother Danny, was getting special treatment from the school because of his parents' status. We all knew it. We all knew they'd made a substantial donation so Danny could get back on the team that fall. It was unfair, and it made my blood boil.

"Cameron and George's teacher tried contacting your mother to explain the situation to her firsthand, but your mother said to talk to you."

"Yeah, she called me…" I trailed off, not wanting to admit I'd ignored her call.

"If you don't mind, sir, I'd like Miss Hamilton to come with me to the elementary school to see Cameron."

Harrison nodded.

"Yes, do that, try to find a solution. I mean, we're talking about six-year-old kids here. I doubt there's any real malice."

Boy, was he wrong. Little kids are the cruelest of all. And I wasn't going to let anything slide until I knew my brother would be safe at school.

Thiago and I left the principal's office.

"Come on, I'll take you to Maggie's class. She told me she needs to talk to a family member, and since you're the only one here…"

"Where is my brother now?" I asked. I desperately needed to give him a hug.

"He's in the teachers' lounge. I told him he could stay there until I got back."

Thiago led me down the long, empty hallways. Everyone else was in class. We kept walking and turned left, through the art wing that connected the high school to the elementary school.

"You know, I stop here sometimes to look at the pictures, and I always wonder if there might be one by you," Thiago said, trying to help me relax.

I'd often looked at those walls, yearning to put up one of my own drawings or paintings, but I'd never mustered the courage.

"Nope," I said with a shrug.

Finally, we reached the double doors that led to the younger kids' classrooms. As soon as I was there, the difference between my brother's school and mine was apparent. The walls were painted bright colors, unlike the gray and white I was used to. The walls were lined with kids' drawings and hooks for little coats and backpacks.

My brother had just started first grade. When Thiago opened the door to the teachers' lounge, I found Cameron curled up on the sofa sleeping, and tears welled in my eyes.

How he must have been suffering, and meanwhile everyone had been punishing him and blaming him for being so strange the last few weeks.

I should never have listened to my mother. If I'd really thought about it, I'd have known that Cam would never be the one to start a fight. It wasn't in his nature.

"Thanks for coming, Kamila," a gentle voice said behind me.

I turned. And I saw her.

There she was: the beautiful woman Thiago had been kissing in front of his house the day before. The same one who had been wearing that tiny miniskirt, passing him his tools and flirting with him.

"I'm Maggie Brown," she said, smiling sweetly and showing off her perfect white teeth. "I'm your brother's teacher. We need to talk."

Seeing her made me want to vomit. Her eyes were sky blue. She was gorgeous. And now she was working side by side with Thiago.

CHAPTER TWO

Kami

"BETTER WE TALK IN MY ROOM," MAGGIE SAID, WAVING ME DOWN the hall to a door with a sign on it that said *The Orangutans*. We walked in and I saw the usual elementary school classroom: pictures drawn in crayon and marker, colorful construction paper, addition and subtraction posters, the alphabet.

"I guess my first question is how things are going at home," she said, leaning on her desk as I sat in a tiny chair. Thiago stood beside her, and I couldn't help but notice how their bodies grazed each other slightly.

"Why do you ask, Maggie?" I couldn't help but call her by her first name. Not when she was probably only five years older than me.

"Your brother's kept to himself since the year started. And that makes his classmates see him as weak, and then they start testing him. Children, you know..."

"Why haven't you done anything to stop them?" I was pissed already. "Principal Harrison said it himself—they're only six. They're babies!"

"I try to let all my students grow at their own pace, and that means encouraging them to explore their identities and—"

"Cut the bullshit. My brother's getting bullied, and nobody's doing anything."

"Kamila," Thiago said, censoring me with his gaze.

I focused my eyes on him. "Don't *Kamila* me!" I practically shouted. "You've known something was going on for weeks, and you didn't bother to tell me? You're my next-door neighbor!"

I don't know why I said that. Maybe to warn Miss Maggie here that she'd better be careful the next time she shows up at her new boyfriend's place in a skimpy skirt. If my brother saw her like that, he could lose all respect for her as a teacher...

"I already told you in the office why I didn't say anything," Thiago said. "I wanted to avoid jumping to conclusions..."

"You took your time, didn't you? How long did you need to realize it's not normal for a six-year-old to be covered in scratches and bruises?"

As soon as the words left my mouth, I realized just how stupid I'd been myself. How could I have just swallowed all his excuses about falling down during soccer, or some game in the blackberry bushes... It was my fault. I had been so focused on myself and my problems and my parents' issues that I hadn't seen the signs...and now it was Cam who was getting hurt.

"Kamila, we *are* going to take action," Maggie told me calmly. "I just need to know if there's anything going on at home that we should know about."

Thiago looked unfazed, but I could tell he was worried.

"My parents are getting a divorce," I admitted, avoiding Thiago's gaze as I said it. I didn't want to see him relishing my misfortune. He'd told me more than once that he wished my family would fall apart the way his had. Maggie, meanwhile, was looking at me with such pity that I wanted to shout, *Wipe that stupid look off your face.* But I kept going. "So as you can imagine, my brother's not exactly living in what you'd call a healthy environment right now."

"I had a hunch," Maggie said, "when I saw this drawing your brother did the other day." She opened a desk drawer, pulled out a sheet of paper, and passed it to me. What I saw filled me with grief. It was a group of stick figures. I guessed that the one on the left was supposed to be my mom. She was bigger than the others and far away from them. She had green circles for eyes, which I realized were probably supposed to represent the cucumbers she put on her eyelids at the spa. On the other side was Dad—I could tell because of his huge belly. He had his back turned, and a phone was pressed to his ear. Cam was in the middle with his iguana. And then there was me. I was tiny, with short blond hair, a giant frown on my face, and blue tears pouring from my eyes.

Was that how my brother saw me?

Was that how he saw all of us?

I could barely bring myself to look up. Thiago was clearly worried, his hand clenched into a fist. "Kids...really suffer when their parents split up," he said. "They hold it all in. That's probably why he didn't tell you about everything that's been going on."

"What's the solution, then?" I asked in a near-whisper.

"I'd like to talk to your parents," Maggie responded, "but they've both made it clear that neither of them can meet with me anytime soon. Some of the kids have told Cam that his father's a thief—that's one of the reasons why I was asking about his home situation."

"Thief?" I interrupted her, taking a moment to understand. "Who said that?"

Maggie, looking uncomfortable, glanced over at Thiago. "George said something about your father stealing a bunch of money from his—"

"That's a lie."

"I understand, but I have to tell you what I've overheard."

I stood, ready to go. There could only be one person behind all this. "I've told you everything you need to know," I said, but before I could go, Maggie turned to me.

"It would be great if you could stop by the playground during recess sometime, just to say hi to Cameron."

"Oh, you better believe I'll be showing up at recess," I said, feeling surer than ever, "and I'll slap the shit out of anyone who dares to lay a finger on my little brother."

After saying that, I rushed off down the hall.

"Kamila!" Thiago shouted when I was a good fifty feet away.

I stopped, took a deep breath, and turned. "What do you want?"

In just a few long strides, he had reached me. "You can't just tell a teacher that you're planning on slapping a bunch of little kids. Are you out of your mind?"

"If no one else is going to stop them, I damn sure will."

"That's not how you do things."

"It isn't? How do you do it then? Jog my memory."

Thiago looked up and down the hall, then gripped my arm and pulled me behind a column next to the janitor's closet.

"Just calm down, OK?" he said, his green eyes gleaming. "I'll make sure no one touches him again."

I'd wanted to tell him to fuck off, but now he had my attention. "Are you serious?" I asked.

He nodded, looking at me like a concerned doctor. "Are you all right?" he said, keeping his eyes on mine.

I felt a tingle in my fingertips, and I wanted to reach up, wrap my hands around his neck, pull him to me and feel those lips on mine.

"Never better," I replied coldly.

"I'm sorry about your parents," he said, and I laughed bitterly.

"Don't insult my intelligence," I told him, stepping back. "You wanted this. Or have you forgotten how much you hate my family?"

Thiago blinked, and I could see that old rage return. "I'll never forget that your mother's selfishness killed my little sister. You can believe that. But I never wanted anything bad to happen to you or your brother."

I couldn't believe what he'd just said. And that made me wish he would touch me even more. Hold me. Kiss me. Before I knew what I was doing, I had stood on my tiptoes and was resting my hand on his chest.

But Thiago stopped me. His hands were on my waist, but he was pushing me back rather than pulling me in. "No," he said. "We can't do this. For all kinds of reasons. Most importantly, you're with my fucking brother."

I pulled away as if his skin were hot metal. My eyes filled with tears. I was a horrible person.

Thiago looked at me, regretful for a moment, then decisive. "Listen, any questions you have about what's going on with Cameron, just ask...but if it's anything else, I'd prefer you keep your distance."

And before I knew it, he'd turned and walked away.

I went to talk to my brother, telling him I was aware of what was going on and that I couldn't understand why he hadn't told me earlier.

"I didn't want to be a snitch..."

I had taken Cam over by the football field, after persuading one of the cafeteria ladies to give me an ice cream sandwich for him. We sat on the lawn, listening to the elementary kids playing soccer in the distance.

"Cam, you're not a snitch, OK? No one has a right to hurt you. No one. You hear me?"

He wouldn't even look me in the eye. He pretended to be interested in the soccer game, but I could tell he wasn't actually watching.

"Cam…" I took a deep breath. "It's sad that Mom and Dad are going to split up. And if you need to talk about it with me, you can. I'm sad too, you know?"

He looked up at me. "You are?"

"Of course." I hated seeing him like that. "But sometimes it's better for people to break up. You don't want to see them fighting all the time, do you?"

He pulled out a few blades of grass and threw them. "I don't want Dad to be alone," he said, tears in his eyes.

My heart shrank. I grabbed him and hugged him as tight as I could. "Dad won't be alone," I said as I felt him break down in sobs. "We'll visit him every weekend. And you know what? When we do, we can stay up past midnight watching *Star Wars* because Mom won't be around to tell us to go to bed!"

Cam turned to me and tried to grin through his tears. "All of them? Can we have a marathon?"

I laughed. "Yes, we can have a marathon."

That seemed to cheer him up. Mom was so controlling. I thought a little less order in his life would probably do him good.

We talked a while longer, and then I took him to class and made it back across campus just in time to grab my books before English class.

"How's it going?" Taylor asked me when I walked through the door. We sat together in all the classes we shared. I don't know if it was the best thing, because I was easily distracted and Taylor was one hell of a distraction. His hand seemed to constantly seek out my inner thigh, though I always stopped him. I couldn't take another visit to the principal's office. But Taylor was surprisingly smart. I remember the teacher once caught us giggling and thought he was going to stump us with a super difficult question about Lenin. But Taylor answered without hesitation, and the teacher had no choice but to go on with his lesson.

One rainy afternoon, when we were sitting in Taylor's car, I had asked him what he wanted to study at college, and he had surprised me by telling me he wanted to be an astronaut. When he saw the look on my face, wide-eyed, he'd started laughing like crazy and said, "You don't believe me? I'm lying. Really, I want to be a computer engineer."

I hadn't expected that either. "How come?" I'd asked.

"So I can hack into all the porn sites without having to pay."

I knew he was kidding. Taylor might be lots of things, but he wasn't a porn addict. I rolled my eyes, and he chuckled again. That was just Taylor—he always blurted out the craziest thing he could come up with, but I liked it because I never got bored with him. I had been so much more easygoing when I was young. But now, all the rules, all the keeping up appearances had made me boring, well-behaved, someone who always obeyed orders and never said "To hell with it."

Taylor was helping me to become bolder, teaching me to live life with no limits, that a day without laughter was a day without meaning, and that there was always something we could do to make ourselves feel better.

Where did you run off to earlier? he wrote in his notebook.

As I read it, I wished I'd opened up to him before. About my parents, about everything. I could have rested my head on his shoulder and let him console me. I was so sad...I took a deep breath and held back the tears.

"Ouch, something's stung me on my foot!" Taylor shouted out of nowhere, right in the middle of class. Everyone turned to stare. I would have believed him if he hadn't winked at me slyly when no one was looking.

"What?" the teacher asked alarmed.

"Something stung me! God, it hurts!"

"Like a wasp or something? Do you want to go to the nurse's office?"

"I don't know, sir, but it's killing me!" Taylor made a show of standing on one leg, and continued with his act of the century. "Help, Kami, please," he said.

I stood and wrapped an arm around him.

"What if I'm allergic?" he exclaimed, putting his hands around his neck.

"Go straight to the nurse, Di Bianco. Hamilton, can you help him on your own?"

"I think so," I said, struggling not to laugh as we walked out.

Once Mr. Stow could no longer see us, Taylor grabbed my hand and took off running.

"What are you doing?" I couldn't believe the stunt he'd just pulled.

We ran down the hall and outside. He dragged me all the way to the bleachers, then underneath. There, he grabbed my face in both hands and gave me a kiss that took my breath away.

"I'm taking care of you. That's what I'm doing," he said. "Now tell me what's wrong."

I could only hold his stare for a second before I broke down in tears.

CHAPTER THREE

Taylor

I HAD KNOWN FOR WEEKS THAT SOMETHING WASN'T RIGHT AT Kami's house. Everyone had heard about their money problems by then. I hated all the gossip about her. Lots of people called Kami *Little Miss Perfect* and were relishing her downfall, and Kami knew it too. She wasn't stupid. The fact that she'd become distanced from her friends wasn't helping matters. Only Ellie kept trying to stay close, concerned whether everything was OK.

I didn't like Kami isolating herself, and it seemed she was doing it more and more. At least I was one of the lucky ones she still let in. But I knew she needed her friends too. Maybe not that idiot Kate, but her other friends would have been a good distraction.

I knew I had to get Kami out of there when I saw how sad she looked in English class. Maybe the bee sting act was overkill, but it had come out of nowhere. We could get busted, worst-case scenario, but I didn't care. I'd be the one to get in trouble, not Kami. And Kami was the only thing that mattered to me. I hugged her, her body seeming to melt into mine as she shook with sobs. "Hey, it's OK," I said, stroking her hair and back.

I don't know how long she cried, but when she finally pulled herself together, she seemed more exhausted than before.

"Sorry," she said, wiping her face and looking at my shirt, which was damp with her tears.

"You can use me as a handkerchief whenever you want," I said, and when I smiled at her, she actually smiled back.

"It's just, everything's been so hard, you know," she said. And then she went into detail about her parents' divorce, their financial situation, her worries about college, and how Danny Walker's brother was bullying Cameron.

"I'd like to beat the shit out of that guy," I said, furious.

Kam shook her head. "Stay out of it, Taylor, please," she said, running her hand across the soft grass. "I need to take care of this on my own."

"If you want my advice, a kick in the nuts should do the trick."

She shook her head and giggled. "I'm going to talk to Danny. Not that I think it will get me anywhere. I need to keep an eye on my brother. Look for the signs. Kids, you know, they can be so good at hiding stuff. I mean, this has been going on for two months and we had no idea."

"I'll talk to Thiago," I said. "Now that he's working with the kids, he should—"

"I already talked to him," she admitted, and I felt a stab in the chest when I thought of the two of them together. "He told me he's going to keep an eye out."

"When did you two talk?" I asked, hoping she wouldn't notice the tension in my voice.

"He was the one who realized what was going on. He took me to talk to Cam's teacher. Maggie, I think, is her name." I couldn't help but notice her frown as she said that name.

Maggie... I knew all about her. She'd been at our house constantly since Thiago first invited her over a week before.

She was beautiful, and I guess she liked him—I could have done without having to listen to them screwing in the bedroom across the hall—but they seemed to have fun together. That was all she was to Thiago, though…just a pleasant distraction.

"Thiago loves your brother, even if he'd never say it out loud. If he told you he's going to watch out for him, you can believe him."

Kami didn't seem convinced, but at least she'd relaxed enough to tell me what had been going on. I'd been through the same thing, more or less, eight years before: my own parents' divorce, the loss of my four-year-old sister, Dad cheating on Mom and then disappearing, Mom falling into depression.

I missed Dad sometimes. He'd never been a bad father; he was the typical dad who took us camping, drove us to basketball games, and bought fireworks on the Fourth of July.

"There you are!" Ellie interrupted us, sticking her head under the bleachers. "You're not going to believe what happened!"

She made us follow her, and when we got back inside, the halls were filled with people shouting and arguing; others were murmuring in small groups. When Kami and I worked our way past them, we saw what all the commotion was about.

Someone had spray-painted the lockers. *Slut*, one of them read; *douchebag* read another; there were more: *bitch*, *asshole*, *pedophile*. The word *cuck* covered mine. I saw red, forgetting everything else.

"It was you, wasn't it?" someone shouted at Kami from the end of the hall. I turned and saw Danny. *Abuser* was written on his locker. Kam and I watched him approach, and when he was within arm's length, it was all I could do not to punch him in the face.

"What are you talking about?" she shouted.

"Your locker's the only one that didn't get defaced. Some coincidence, huh?"

We looked around, and it was true. Whoever had done it had passed her over on purpose.

"It wasn't me!" she protested.

But Danny's accusation had the desired effect, and soon everyone was shouting at her, including Julian, who scowled and said, "You were the only one who knew!"

Kami shook her head as she looked at Julian's locker, where the word *gay* was written in giant letters.

Wait... Julian was gay? That was something I hadn't expected.

"I swear to God, it wasn't me!" Kami shouted, walking backward. She bumped into me, and I wrapped my arms around her, glaring at everyone else.

"Kami was outside with me. She didn't do anything," I said, unable to believe what was happening.

"You're her boyfriend. Of course you'd say that!"

"You always stick up for her!"

Danny mumbled a few words under his breath that I couldn't hear, but they clearly terrified Kami, so I did something I'd been wanting to do for weeks. I punched him straight in the mouth, sending him to the floor.

An announcement came over the PA: *All students to the gymnasium immediately! I repeat, all students to the gym immediately!*

Danny got up and brought his face close to mine just as the crowd started to disperse. "Touch me again, Di Bianco," he said, "and it'll be the last thing you ever do."

Kami got between us before I could challenge him. "Taylor, please," she said, "don't let him get to you." Her voice trembled, making me look back at her, the only person I really cared about just then. Screw Danny.

I grabbed her hand. "We should get to the gym."

Everyone was scowling at us. More at Kami than at me. When we reached the gym, the bleachers were full and everyone was silent. Kami's anxiety was palpable, and I was angry, knowing that she had another worry on her plate. Who was setting her up, and why?

The principal came in, along with the rest of the teachers. He stood in the middle of the gym, grabbed the microphone, and began to speak.

"I'm sure all of you have seen the hallways. I don't know who thought this was a funny prank, but we don't tolerate this sort of thing around here. This is without a doubt the worst act of vandalism we've ever seen at this school. We've always been proud of having the kind of student body where we didn't need surveillance cameras or security personnel, where we didn't have to conduct investigations. Well, I guess that's over. But let me promise you all something: We will find the person who did this, and not only will they be expelled, they will pay for the cost of repainting the lockers. We're looking at thousands of dollars in damages, and they'd better be ready to pay every cent of it. Now, I'm going to make an offer, but only this once: If whoever did this comes to my office and confesses, their punishment will be less severe. I'll consider suspension instead of expulsion. I will not tolerate this type of behavior. Is that clear?"

No one dared to respond.

"Now get back to class."

Everyone filed out, but once we were in the halls, the whispering and gossiping started up again. I could see Kami getting more and more nervous every time she overheard her name. I pushed her into the handicapped bathroom and locked the door. "Kami, you were with me, and Ellie is our witness. People aren't going to blame you once they find out, I promise."

"Who do you think did it, though? Why would someone want to make me look bad?"

"People are jealous of you, babe." I stroked her cheek. "They want to see you fall, and they're trying to make it happen."

"I'll fall if that's what they want. I don't care. I just want to be left alone."

"Trust me. I'll make sure they leave you alone."

I kissed her, and we opened the door and walked to biology class.

Everyone glared at us when we walked in late, except for Kate, who didn't even look up when we passed her. The rest of the day was a nightmare. I spent it trying to convince people that Kami was innocent, that she had been with me the entire time. Some of the guys believed me, but most sided with Danny Walker, and for him, this was the perfect excuse to get even more people to hate his ex-girlfriend. How pathetic could one guy be?

At practice, things got worse. Kami was home by then since our detention had finally ended and she had quit the cheerleading squad. I'd seen her outside, waiting for her dad in the bitter cold. I told her I'd drive her home and hurry back to practice, but I knew it would make me late, and she insisted that she was happy out there, that the cold cleared her head, and that she needed a little time on her own to think.

During warm-up, Thiago grabbed Danny by the arm and pulled him into a corner. No one seemed to notice, they were too busy practicing free throws, but I listened in.

"You keep spreading these rumors and I'll bench you until Judgment Day, get it?"

Danny pulled away from Thiago and smiled moronically.

"Your days are numbered, *Coach*," he responded, walking backward and glancing over at me. "You be careful too," he said to me. "You don't want him walking off with your girlfriend."

After that, Danny rejoined the team. I froze, trying to take his words in before looking at my brother, who was still staring at Danny. "What was that supposed to mean?" I asked him.

"He's a dumbass," Thiago said calmly. "That's what it's supposed to mean. Now keep practicing those jump shots."

I held his stare for a moment and then let it go. I wasn't going to dwell on the thought, even if it had been nagging me for weeks.

Kami wouldn't do that.

Kami wouldn't cheat on me, and my brother sure as hell wouldn't let her.

CHAPTER FOUR

Kami

HOW COULD EVERYTHING FALL APART SO FAST? SINCE THE SCHOOL year had started, everything had gone from bad to worse. Even if they'd brought me problems, Thiago and Taylor being back was my one saving grace. Knowing they were next door again, seeing their mother leaving for work, was something I could only have dreamed a year ago.

The day had drawn on so long, I thought it would never end. First I'd found out about my brother, then Thiago had rejected me, and besides—how could I be so stupid as to try to kiss him? What the hell was I thinking? We'd both agreed it was over between us. It had to be. I knew that.

I was with *Taylor*.

Taylor...and I loved him, dammit! Even on that horrible day, he'd managed to wring a smile out of me. But then the thing with the lockers happened. Why would someone do that? Who had wanted to turn everyone against me? Someone hated me. That much was certain.

Now the whole school thought I'd spray-painted the seniors' lockers. Julian had even fallen for it, and now he didn't trust me, and our friendship was ruined. I had to talk to him.

I got home around four. As far back as I can remember, I'd never gotten home that early unless practice had been canceled for some reason or we had a half day. But I had to admit, it was nice having a little time for myself now that I'd quit the squad. I could study for hours, and I wouldn't have to stay up all night to get good grades. I could even draw or read a book without feeling guilty about not doing something more productive with my time. Quitting cheerleading had opened up a new world to me. And best of all, I didn't have to spend so much time at school.

When we walked into the house, we found Mom and Dad sitting at the coffee table across from a man in his fifties with gray hair and a white beard. There was a stack of papers in front of them.

"How was school?" Mom asked, looking up from the papers she was reading.

"Good," I lied, keeping my eyes on the stranger. "What are you doing?"

"This is Mr. Richards, my lawyer," my mother said, a little too politely. "He's drawn up a draft of the divorce agreement, and we're going over it together."

I couldn't believe how coolly she could talk about splitting up with the man she'd been with since she was nineteen years old. This was the first time I'd seen Dad not looking sad or bitter. He just seemed serious, as though he'd accepted it. Had he finally seen Mom's true colors?

I was furious, and it was hard to control my feelings. But for my own good, I needed to remain calm. I stepped forward and directly addressed the lawyer, "Mr. Richards," I said as politely as I could muster. "What do I have to do to be able to live with my father?"

Mr. Richards looked back and forth uncomfortably between my parents.

"Well, um…it says here your parents have agreed that you and your brother will be staying with your mother for now, and—"

"I'm eighteen, though, so I can choose, right?"

"Kamila…" my mother said nervously.

"According to the law, you're an adult, so it's your right. But let's not forget the question of who is willing or able to support you. Your parents have told me you're still in high school—"

"But if I get a job I can go, right?"

"Kamila," Dad said sternly, "that's enough. You're staying with your mother. We've talked it over. It's decided."

I turned to him. "Why?" I asked, hurt. "Don't you want me to live with you?"

He took a deep breath and pinched the bridge of his nose.

"What I want is for you to stay with your brother, Kamila," he said, looking bitter. He'd made his decision.

That made me reconsider things.

"He's still little, and he needs to be with your mother. Cam needs you now too, even more than ever."

"Plus," my mother chimed in, daring me to talk back to her, "I'll need you to look after him when I'm busy."

"Oh, I get it. You want me to live with you so I can play babysitter?"

Mr. Richards seemed uncomfortable but intrigued, moving his head left and right like someone watching a tennis match.

"Your father doesn't have the means to provide for us anymore. Don't you see that?" my mother asked, losing her composure.

"And you do?"

"Your grandparents are going to help us out."

Oh, God. Just what I needed. "So that's it. You'd rather go running to your parents than try to look for a job yourself." I didn't give one shit that the lawyer was witnessing all this.

My father turned to him. "Mr. Richards, I think it would be best we leave this for another day."

The lawyer stood, gathered his things, and stuffed them into his briefcase. "Of course. We can speak tomorrow," he said, unable to hide the annoyed look on his face.

I wasn't going to stick around and talk with them. I turned, ready to go to my room and lock the door, but Mom stopped me. "Kamila, this is over," she said. "I'm not going to put up with this spoiled attitude from you any longer."

"Well, if you want me to live with you, you'd better get used to it," I responded.

"Roger, do something!" she shouted to my father.

"Sorry, I'm not going to be a part of this stupid argument. Kamila, you're too old for these hissy fits. You did say one thing that made sense, though—you really ought to look for a job, given the circumstances."

My jaw dropped. "You can't be serious," I said.

"What your mother said was true. I'm broke. I can't pay for this house *and* your expenses, at least not for a while. We only have enough to keep up the mortgage through the end of the school year. But I can't keep up with your allowance."

"Roger, I told you my parents would help us. Kamila doesn't need to go flip burgers. She'll be taken care of," Mom said with a defiant look in her eyes, as if wanting to assert that she would take care of us from now on.

"I think I will get a job," I said, without skipping a beat. "Now that I'm not on the cheerleading squad, I can find something part-time that'll still leave me time to study."

"What?" my mother shouted, wide-eyed. "You quit the squad?"

"A couple of weeks ago." I couldn't believe she hadn't figured that out.

"Why?"

"Because I felt like it!" I crossed my arms. "I'd rather use my time to study…or work," I added, realizing that my freedom had lasted exactly fourteen days.

"My goodness, what will they say in town? You quit cheer-leading, get a job… After all those years training, you were the captain, and you're going to quit?"

"Yep," I replied. "Cheerleading is dumb. It's not like there's anything you can do with it after high school. I mean, you were a cheerleader, and what have you ever done?"

Mom tensed up, and I knew I'd crossed a line.

"Kamila, go to your room," Dad said, and I didn't hesitate a second.

Upstairs, I shut the door, sat at my desk, and typed *Carsville help wanted* into the search engine. I spent the rest of the after-noon sending out résumés.

Around six, I was tired, and my eyes were burning after two hours of staring at the screen, so I threw on some leggings, a sweat-shirt, and my headphones and got ready for a run. The cold helped clear my head and made me feel less guilty for mouthing off to my mother. It wasn't her fault she'd been raised to think the entire goal of life was to look perfect and vulnerable and have some man pay for everything. But that wouldn't work for me.

I usually ran farther out of town, but this time I took the opposite route. I jogged into Carsville, with its perfectly paved streets, its trim pines, its redbrick buildings, and its mom-and-pop shops. It had gotten dark, and I could see the customers inside, taking shelter from the cold with a hot cup of coffee or looking at clothes and trinkets, buying produce, or just wandering the aisles killing time before it got too late.

I slowed down to a quick walk.

What was it about this town that made everyone want to be so perfect?

I went to Mill's, the café on the square. I loved that place, loved going in and getting a giant mug of coffee and a fresh-baked brownie and sitting down to draw. It was the best place in town, and everybody went there to meet friends or take a break from their routines. On the weekends it was packed, but during the week you could usually get a seat. It was big, divided up into three spaces. In one, there were tables with plugs where you could work on your computer; that's where the students usually hung out. Then there was the café, with three or four little round tables and the big picture window with views of the street and the square. Finally, there was the section by the pastry cooler, where you could always find Mr. and Mrs. Mill selling their cakes, croissants, rye bread, and cookies.

When I walked in, the bell rang, and the rich scent of chocolate and baking bread hit me. I could hear murmurs and, in the background, the Mill's soundtrack: classic rock, no matter the time of day or year.

"Kami! I haven't seen you in ages!" Mrs. Mill said, warm as always. She was a plump woman in her seventies with tender blue eyes and crow's-feet from laughing all the time. She adored my little brother, and anytime I brought him in, she'd stuff him with sweets.

It wasn't long before she asked after him: "Where's your brother?"

"He's at home, Mrs. Mill." I edged closer to the counter, amused. "How are you? And how's Mr. Mill?"

"I'm great, dear," she said, making change for the woman in line. "Mr. Mill isn't doing so well, though. It's his back. But so it goes. How about you?"

"I'm good, just studying a lot," I said and smiled.

"Getting ready to go to Yale?"

I laughed. "I hope so, Mrs. Mill." I ordered a cappuccino and a slice of her classic carrot cake.

"Go sit down, dear, I'll bring it over to you."

I thanked her and turned around to look for a table. But the first thing I saw was a pair of green eyes. Thiago was sitting there with an empty cup of coffee and his laptop. I hadn't seen him before because he was in the corner, partly concealed by a white column.

I took a deep breath and forced myself to walk over. As our eyes met, I couldn't help but feel butterflies in my stomach. "Listen, Thiago…"

"Have a seat," he said, motioning to the chair across from him.

I hesitated but then sat down. I couldn't help but take a mental snapshot of him: navy-blue shirt with rolled-up sleeves, disheveled hair, unshaven face, penetrating stare. "I wanted to say sorry about this morning."

"You don't have anything to apologize for." He closed his laptop and leaned his elbows on the table, resting his chin in his hands. I felt his eyes bathe me in warmth. "How are you? Today must have been a tough one for you."

I tried to pull my brain back down to earth and formulate an answer. "Fine," I said as Mrs. Mill brought me my coffee and cake, setting both down and saying, "Here you are, honey." After a glance at the two of us, she asked, "Why are you two so glum?"

Thiago sat back in his chair. He probably hated that, a café owner sticking her nose in our business. He couldn't stand small-town life, the gossip, the tedium of people in Carsville.

"Just chatting, Mrs. Mill," I said, since Thiago seemed incapable of filling the silence.

Unruffled, she responded, "Well, that's fine, but I better not hear this boy trying to break your heart, eh?"

"Mrs. Mill!" I covered my face with my hands in embarrassment.

After she walked off, Thiago said, "It's times like this when I remember what I liked so much about DC."

"Does that mean you won't stick around here once the school year's done?"

"Why do you ask? Do you want me to go?"

"I didn't say that," I clarified. "It's just this town... You don't really fit in here."

"And you do?"

I shrugged in response and then said, after a moment's thought, "I don't think I'll stay here forever."

"Yeah, I heard you wanted to go to Yale."

I nodded and took a sip of coffee.

"Why?" he asked, and he seemed genuinely curious.

"To study art."

He nodded. "Let me get this straight, though. You want to study art, but you also hide your talent from absolutely everybody. So what are you going to do when you go to college and you have no choice but to exhibit your work?"

"Isn't college supposed to change you?" I asked hopefully.

"I don't know," he said. "I didn't stay long enough to find out."

I felt sorry for him. He must have had so many plans for his future. And now he was stuck here. The old guilt swelled inside me. *It could have been so different if his sister hadn't died*, I thought. "Aren't you thinking of going back?"

"All I wanted to do was play ball, but no college team will take me with my record."

I knew that was hard for him to admit. Even though he played it cool on the surface, it was eating away at him. "Could you consider studying something else?"

Thiago shook his head, reached over, grabbed my cup, and stole a sip, leaving me speechless. "My brother's more the college type. I don't have what it takes to put up with that shit for four years."

There was no conviction in his words. "You're amazing, Thiago. You could do anything you put your mind to."

His eyes warned me not to push it. "What about you and my brother? How are you going to manage it?"

"Manage what?"

He took a bite of my cake. "I mean, Harvard's in Massachusetts and Yale is in Connecticut."

I hadn't thought about it, and I told him, feeling uncomfortable that we'd never discussed it. I didn't like talking to Thiago about my relationship with Taylor.

"That sure is a long bike ride," he commented with a grin.

He was so handsome, I had to smile back. "Right... I guess I'll need to buy a car. So I'd better start saving." I wrapped my fingers around my mug to warm them up.

"Is your allowance enough for you to buy another one?"

"I don't get an allowance anymore," I admitted.

"Poor thing," he teased.

"I need a job, actually, at least if I'm ever going to do anything more interesting than sit around my house. You haven't heard of any openings, have you?"

"No," he said. "So you're on a job hunt. Looks like you're growing up." He seemed proud.

"You sound like my dad."

"Listen up: Whatever my feelings are for you, I can promise you they're not paternal."

Was that a compliment? "Really, though," I said, "I need work, if you hear of anything."

Thiago took another sip of my coffee, and just as I was about to tell him to get his own, he pointed at something behind me.

I turned. There it was right on the chalkboard with the day's specials: *Help wanted*. I couldn't believe it.

"No shit!"

Thiago opened his laptop, getting back to work, as he murmured, "I'll admit, I do like the idea of you serving me coffee and cookies."

I ignored him and walked to the counter.

"Mrs. Mill," I said, "I hear you're hiring."

She beamed. "That's right, dear. With Mr. Mill not doing well, I need someone to lend a hand around here."

"I could do it," I said enthusiastically.

"You?" She seemed unconvinced.

"Please, Mrs. Mill. I promise I'll be the best employee you've ever had."

She thought it over and replied, "All right then, I'll talk it over with Mr. Mill. You'd have to come in and try it out for a day. But if you can handle it, then why not?"

I smiled so bright it must have lit up the whole café. "Thank you, Mrs. Mill! How about tomorrow afternoon?"

"Sure, dear," she said sweetly. She seemed amused to see me so happy about it.

I walked back to the table, overjoyed, and saw Taylor had shown up and was sitting with his brother.

"Did you get the job?" Taylor asked, looking amused. Thiago was trying to smile along with him, but a shadow had fallen over his face.

"I think so!" I said, approaching them. "When did you get here?"

"While you were over there talking." He reached up, grabbed my hand, and pulled me into his lap. With his brother there, that show of affection felt strange, and I wanted to get up, but I knew that would hurt Taylor's feelings.

"I see you two are talking again," Taylor said, looking back and forth between Thiago and me.

"When you're bored, I guess any ear will do, right?" his brother responded, closing his laptop and gathering his things. "I'll leave you to it."

"Wait, don't go," his brother said, forcing a smile. "Does this mean we're all friends again? Because no one informed me."

"Taylor..." I tried to butt in.

"We're all friends," his brother announced abruptly. "I need to go, though. Is that OK?" He suddenly looked bored.

"Stick around for a while. It won't kill you to hang out with your brother and his girlfriend, will it?"

Oh, Taylor, won't you please shut up!

Thiago sat down and observed us the way someone might stare at a painting.

"So it's official now? You're boyfriend and girlfriend?"

We'd never actually talked about it. People just assumed, and we hadn't corrected them.

"Seems like it," Taylor said and squeezed my waist. In the ensuing silence, I got an uneasy feeling and wished I could think of something to say to make the situation less awkward. But Taylor beat me to it. "I've got an idea!" He smiled. "Remember that time capsule we buried in the yard way back when?"

Thiago tensed up the way he always did when we talked about the old days. "What about it?" he asked, toying with the sugar shaker on the table.

"We should dig it up!"

Thiago put the shaker down and stood. "Sorry, no time."

"Come on, Thiago!"

Looking at the two brothers, I remembered that day as though it were yesterday. We had grabbed our favorite things and stuck them in a metal box we'd bought at the hardware store. And we'd each written a note we were supposed to read ten years later.

"We agreed we'd wait ten years. It's only been eight," Thiago said.

"Who cares?" Taylor objected. "Come on, it'll be fun."

Even I liked the idea. "Why don't we wait and do it on the night of the Halloween party?" I suggested. "We buried it on Halloween, right? So it'll be like an anniversary."

"Yeah," Taylor responded, clearly happy I was enthusiastic about it too.

Thiago wasn't, though. His mood had gone from skeptical to hostile, or so I thought until his frown turned into a grin and he grumbled, "You two are still a couple of babies. But fuck it. I'll go just to make sure you don't dig the hole too deep and fall in."

Taylor and I laughed.

"Friday at seven, by the tree house then?" Taylor said.

Thiago and I both nodded. I felt the same excitement from long ago at the thought of a new adventure. But this time, it would be with two incredibly attractive guys. And I had something going on with both of them. Even if I didn't know exactly what it was.

CHAPTER FIVE

Kami

THE REST OF THE WEEK WAS WEIRD. EVERYONE WAS TENSE BECAUSE of the thing with the lockers. Some people believed me when I said I'd been with Taylor when it happened, especially after Ellie told them she'd found us outside talking under the bleachers. Others said they'd seen me do it and my boyfriend and my best friend were just covering for me. It was ridiculous, but it didn't really surprise me.

The worst thing was when Kate came over during my free period along with all my former friends to tell me they were done with me. "It was bad enough how you let us down when the team needed you most, but writing *wannabe* on my locker when you know how hard I worked for years to be the team captain, that's just low—cruel *and* childish."

"I didn't do it," I said, trying to remain calm.

"Oh, so it's just a coincidence that someone wrote *ass kissers* on the other cheerleaders' lockers. You think we honestly believe you're our friend and you wouldn't do that?" Marissa asked. That stung.

"It wasn't me!"

"Whatever," Kate said. Then she scowled at Ellie. "I expected more out of you, Galadriel."

"Don't call me that."

"You two were made for each other," Kate responded, shaking her head. "I honestly can't believe I used to think you were my closest friends."

With those words, I saw a glimmer of what looked like real emotion in her brown eyes, then she turned and walked away. When had Kate become such a horrible person? Where was my lifelong friend?

"Kami, don't listen to them, seriously," Ellie said, trying to make me feel better. But she, too, had been hurt by the way our friends were stabbing us in the back. "Ever since she was named captain, Kate's been on this ego trip..."

"Quitting that stupid squad is the best thing I've ever done."

Ellie was still on the squad, though, and getting along with her teammates had become impossible. The one thing that saved us was Taylor. His being my boyfriend gave us a layer of protection because, despite everything, he was still the cute boy, captain of the basketball team, and half the girls were madly in love with him.

The guys didn't seem to care about the whole locker thing as much as the girls. Some of them even thought it was funny. The exception was Danny. The fact that he'd been so upset at being called an *abuser* and then immediately blamed me made it clear: he was everything he'd been accused of.

I hadn't talked to anyone about what he'd done, not even Ellie, but he had taken things too far with me more than once. And I was so stupid, I had forgiven him because I felt pressure to keep going out with the most popular guy in school and I didn't want to disappoint my parents. Plus, it was hard for me to admit that I had let someone treat me that way. And then there was always the question of whether anyone would have believed me if I'd told them what had happened.

But then Taylor started asking questions about it one day after class. We'd just blended chicken liver with detergent to see its DNA—gross, but interesting too. Taylor had loved it, he was like a mad scientist, laughing so much the teacher had to reprimand us like five times. Afterward, as we stood talking outside, he told me how he couldn't stop thinking about the lockers and especially what had been written on Danny Walker's. It had stopped raining for once, and though it was cold, it was nice to see the sunshine. We walked to a picnic table, Tay sat down, and I stood there between his legs. Remembering what had happened between Danny and me. I tensed up and looked away.

But Taylor grabbed my chin and forced me to look him in the eye. "Did he hurt you, Kami?"

I didn't want to talk about it. And I didn't want him to know because there was nothing that could come of it, apart from another fight.

"Can we not talk about Danny?" I asked calmly. "Why don't you tell me what you're going to be for Halloween?"

"Don't change the subject."

"Taylor, I don't want to talk about it because if I do, it's gonna cause..."

His body instantly tensed up like a guitar string, tuned and ready to play a loud note. "What did he do to you?"

"Nothing!" I lied, trying to sound convincing. "Seriously, can you drop it?"

"I promise you I won't start a fight. I just want to know what that asshole is capable of."

I took a deep breath. "He doesn't know his own strength... We'd get in fights sometimes, and he'd grab my arms, and he'd just squeeze too hard."

"I'm going to kill him," Taylor said, starting to get up.

Seeing his reaction confirmed what I already knew. "See, Taylor?" I said, grabbing his shirt and pulling him back. "I knew I couldn't tell you anything."

"How do you expect me to just sit back and do nothing when I know that he hurt you?"

"It's the past, Taylor, and it needs to stay there. It's my business, and I took care of it the best I could."

But it hadn't ended there. Because now Danny's brother was involved, and my brother too. I'd stopped by to see him for a second that day at recess. He had seemed OK. The teachers were keeping an eye on him, and I hadn't noticed any more scratches or bruises.

"What are *you* dressing up as for Halloween?" Taylor finally asked after sitting there for a few moments in sullen silence.

"Honestly? No idea." I hadn't even thought about it. And it's not like I had any money to spend on a costume or time to make one. I'd have to improvise. "Honestly, the way things have been going, I'm not sure if Aaron's party is even a good idea for me. I don't really want to show up just to give everyone a chance to glare at me like I'm some sort of witch."

"You know what?" he responded suddenly, looking convinced. "Screw Aaron's party. We'll see who can really draw the people in. I'll throw a party at my house, and people won't dare give you dirty looks. I think I've made it clear at this point: Anyone who messes with you messes with me."

I smiled and pulled him toward me, tugging at his shirt.

"You're doing it again," I said, brushing his lips with mine. "I know how to take care of myself."

I don't think he heard my words before he started kissing me. Taylor was a good kisser: he knew how to bring me to my knees and make me feel like no one could ever hurt me as long as I was in his arms. He was the kind of guy who would take a bullet for the people he cared about. And dammit…that was going to be his downfall.

———————

My training shift at Mill's was a success. I mean, it wasn't a secret to anyone that cakes and cookies were kind of my thing. I'd won competitions at the county fair, and my cakes were always the first to sell out, and that fact convinced Mrs. Mill. I could wait tables and cash people out at the counter, and I was more than happy to bake anything she asked.

"Now if you see a bunch of kids come in here to drink nothing but water or split one coffee between them, as if this were some sort of library, you let me know," she said. "I'll go over and start lecturing them about the war. You just watch how they scamper off like scared little lizards. Teenagers today, they don't give a damn about anything but TikTak and Pinstagram."

It cracked me up that she couldn't remember what TikTok was called and that she thought Instagram and Pinterest were the same thing, but now I knew her secret weapon. I had done the very thing she was complaining about. This was a business, after all, and plenty of times we'd come in just to study and read, it was so comfortable in there.

Combining school and work ended up being easier than I'd thought. If it was a slow night, Mrs. Mill would let me study behind the counter. One downside was having to serve my own classmates. They couldn't believe that the former queen of the school, who had always had money and used to take European vacations every summer, was now slinging coffee. I heard their remarks, and I tried to ignore their laughter when I had my back turned.

My mother hated seeing her daughter work in *that dump*, as she called it. She had lied to her friends at the club, telling them the job would look good on my application to Yale. It was stupid—anyone who didn't live under a rock had heard about our financial problems by now. Mom had lost her power. And she wasn't handling it well.

On Friday afternoon, Julian came in and took a table in the corner. We looked at each other warily, and when I walked over to ask if I could get him anything, he asked me to sit down. I looked over at Mrs. Mill, noticed there was no one in line, and decided to join him for a moment.

"I'm sorry, Kam," he said, calling me by the nickname only Thiago used for me. "I know it wasn't you. I know you'd never do something like that. But when I saw that word on my locker, I couldn't think. I just reacted."

"It's fine. I understand. I really do," I said, pleased to see he no longer blamed me.

"It wasn't right. I was a bad friend. I have been for weeks now," he said, taking my hand. "I know things haven't been easy for you. You pulled away from me and everyone else, and I thought you didn't want to be my friend anymore."

"Of course I still want to be your friend, Julian! But what you're saying is true. I did pull away. And I think now they see me as weak."

"People might think you're a nobody now that your little gang's rejected you," he responded indignantly. "But they're wrong."

"That little gang was all my friends. And they won't even speak to me."

"They weren't your friends then. They have no idea about the kind of person you are, Kam. You *are* the queen of the school, you always will be, and people will realize that whether they want to or not."

I shook my head and let go of his hands. "That doesn't matter to me anymore," I said, fiddling with the dish towel in my hand. "It's true that I don't like the way they're all looking at me, and

I don't like being accused of things I didn't do, but I never liked being the center of attention. Now that I'm not, I can just be me, you know?"

"Kam, if you're going out with Taylor Di Bianco, you *are* the center of attention."

I shrugged. "I can't help it. He's my boyfriend. If people don't like it, fuck them." This was the first time I'd publicly acknowledged my relationship with Taylor.

"Well, well, well," he said, and his eyes got wider. "You've finally confirmed it. Now I want all the dirty details. What's his package like?"

I was blushing, since I had no idea what the answer was.

"Don't tell me you haven't done it!" Julian exclaimed.

I shook my head, uncomfortable. Julian was going too far. That was private; it was between me and Taylor and no one else. "Not yet."

He shook his head. "What are you waiting for? He's hot."

"I don't know," I said. "We just haven't had the chance."

"But do you want to?"

I thought it over. "I don't know if I'm ready yet."

"Are you still a virgin?" he asked in a near-whisper. I couldn't believe how nosy he was!

"No, but I don't see why that's relevant."

"Don't tell me Danny Walker is the only guy who's had the privilege?!"

"Julian! Can we please stop talking about my sex life?"

He raised his hands in surrender. "Sorry, sorry." But he looked amused. His expression changed from sly to tender as he smiled and said, "I missed you."

"Me too," I said. Just then the doorbell chimed. It was Taylor and Thiago. They eyed us suspiciously, and I stood, hearing Julian beside me say, "Love comes calling."

"Shut up," I hissed, walking back to the counter. With a smile, I asked the two of them if they wanted anything.

"Yeah," Thiago said.

"You," Taylor added, acting like his brother wasn't standing right there. I blushed again. Why did his saying that in front of Thiago make me feel guilty? Almost like I was cheating... I know it sounds ridiculous.

"I guess you heard this idiot is throwing a party at our house tomorrow?" Thiago said.

"Yeah, a Halloween party." I nodded.

"Well, we were heading out to buy decorations and..."

"What Tay's trying to say is your brother jumped into the back seat of our car and he insists we take him with us," Thiago continued. "I kept saying no, but he wouldn't budge, so finally we decided to drive over here and leave him with you so you can take him home when you're done with your shift."

Taylor frowned at his brother. "Actually, we came to ask if you wanted to come so the four of us could do it together. Incidentally, though, I will say your little brother can be persuasive when he wants to."

"He didn't persuade me of a damn thing," Thiago said.

I frowned. That was weird, my brother just getting into someone else's car. "You'd better just leave him here," I responded. "I'll be off in twenty minutes."

"Great, then we'll just wait for you," Taylor said.

"I don't know if that's a good idea," I said.

"Why not?" Taylor crossed his arms. He was as stubborn as my little brother.

"Uh..." I couldn't think of a decent excuse.

"I thought so," Taylor shot back. "That settles it. You're coming." He went out to the car to get my brother.

"You could have made up some excuse," Thiago said.

I sighed. "Let me get you a coffee while you wait."

I walked behind the counter to greet a couple who had just walked in, Taylor and Cam behind them. As the three of them settled in at a table, Julian stood, waved, and came to say goodbye. I was sneakily pouring chocolate syrup into a steaming pitcher—my brother loved hot chocolate, and I knew Mrs. Mill would want me to charge him for it, which I couldn't bring myself to do.

"You've got a whole entourage of guys today, don't you?" Julian said.

"I don't know how I do it," I said, smiling at my three favorite people in the world. Why lie? I liked seeing them together. I was glad we were all getting along again, the old gang, even despite what had happened in Thiago's car a few weeks back.

"Sure," Julian said, looking back at them. "Listen, let's grab a coffee sometime, OK?"

"You got it."

Julian paid, and as he left, I noticed both Taylor and Thiago staring at him. He waved at them, and Taylor responded in kind, while Thiago ignored him.

"Can we go now?" Cam asked, hopping up and down in his seat.

"I need another minute," I said, going into the back to hang up my apron and grab my things. I said goodbye to Mrs. Mill, and the four of us walked to the car. Thiago got in the driver's seat, and Cam and I sat in the back.

"Can I go to your guys' party?" he asked.

"No," Thiago and I said in unison. Taylor, though, shouted, "Hell yeah!" I narrowed my eyes at him, and he changed his tune. "I mean, you can help us set up. But you can't stay for the party. Sorry, pal. It's for grown-ups."

"How is it for grown-ups if it's a costume party?" Cam asked.

"Older people dress up too," Taylor replied.

"Not me," Thiago murmured as he put on his turn signal and took a right. It was dark, and there was lots of traffic, mostly people headed home to the suburbs. We were going to the Walmart in the next town over—Carsville didn't have any big-box stores.

"Whatever. If you're dressing up, I am too," Cameron protested, crossing his arms.

"Sure, man, I'll dress up with you, and we'll put up the decorations together. It'll be super Halloweenish!"

"Is that even a real word?" asked my know-it-all brother. I laughed, and Taylor shrugged.

"I like making up words. Where do you think languages come from anyway?"

"But to be a real word, it has to be used by lots of people. Isn't that right, Kami?" Cameron asked.

"I guess so."

"So let's all start using it, and it'll become one!"

Thiago had to rain on his parade. "You try using the word *Halloweenish* with your teacher and see what kind of grade you get."

Taylor turned and winked at us, and Cam smiled as we got out of the car.

My brother clung to Taylor like a leech as they walked through the aisles filling up the cart. I hung back with Thiago.

"Those two," he said. "If you didn't know better, you'd think they were brothers." He grabbed a couple of tools from a floor display. I could tell he didn't give a shit about Halloween. He had just used the trip as an excuse to get stuff for his motorcycle or some other project.

"I wish I could keep holding on to that childlike innocence," I said.

"Yeah," Thiago responded. "I haven't felt that for a long time." There was bitterness in his tone.

I remembered we were supposed to open our time capsule the next day before the party, and my stomach did a flip. It brought back all the times we'd snuck out at night to have adventures. I was excited to finally do that again with the two guys who had been like brothers to me.

Taylor and Cam reappeared with a full cart. Taylor had gotten cotton spiderwebs, giant spiders to hang from the trees, ghosts, fake blood, candy, cups with monsters on them, eerie lights, even one of those dumb speakers that makes a scary noise whenever you walk by it. "They're having a fifty percent off sale," Taylor said, shrugging.

Thiago didn't say anything. After we'd checked out, he grabbed six of the bags and took them to the car. Taylor, Cameron, and I divided up the rest. When we parked at their house, Cam reminded Taylor that he'd be by early to help set everything up.

"Sounds cool," Taylor said. I grabbed my little brother's hand and said goodbye to Thiago. Taylor came over to give me a kiss on the cheek. "See you tomorrow, precious," he said and winked. I smiled and dragged Cameron home.

As soon as we'd closed the door behind us, he asked, "Kami, is Taylor your boyfriend?" I tried to tell him to zip it, but before I could, Mom walked out of the kitchen. I had texted her to let her know Cam was with me. She hadn't even noticed he was gone or that he'd run off to the neighbor's house.

"Did I hear the word *boyfriend*?" she asked suspiciously.

"No," I replied.

"She's got one, Mom. It's Taylor Di Bianco!" Cam screamed. *Shit.*

With daggers in her eyes, my mother said, "You *are kidding* me, right?"

I wondered whether I should lie to her, but it was probably too late. And anyway, I was tired of hiding. "We're dating," I admitted, and waited for trouble to come. But Mom was silent for a moment.

"You're grounded," she finally said.

"What? Now you're kidding, right?"

"Cameron," she said, "go take a shower. Dinner will be ready in ten minutes."

My brother looked at my mother and then at me, and I could tell he was happy to get away. He ran off up the stairs, and Mom spun around and went back to the kitchen.

"You can't punish me for having a boyfriend," I said, hot on her heels.

"I can punish you for whatever reason I feel like."

"You can, huh? Then you better buy a padlock and shut me in my room because there's no way I'm staying home just because you tell me to."

Mom stopped stirring whatever she had in the pot and looked at me in a fury. "It's not enough that I'm getting a divorce! It's not enough that your father's broke! No! You have to go out with the last person your father and I would ever want to see you with!"

"Can you stop making everything about you? This is my life! I'm having a hard time too! And in case you forgot, Taylor and Thiago used to be my best friends before you screwed everything up and they had to move away!"

"Well, you can kiss them both goodbye because this is not happening, not as long as you're under my roof."

"Sure, Mom, you screw their dad and that means I can't be Taylor's girlfriend? Sorry, that's not how it works. Taylor *is* my boyfriend, and the sooner you get used to the idea, the better."

Without waiting for a response, I turned on my heels and walked up to my room.

CHAPTER SIX

Thiago

"I WASN'T EXPECTING YOU TODAY," MAGGIE SAID, OPENING THE door to her apartment downtown.

I hadn't been expecting to visit her either, but I desperately needed to get out of the house.

I couldn't stand the sight of my brother. I actually felt like I wanted to fight him. And what was I supposed to do when I felt that way about someone I loved so much?

This was fucked. I was fucked. Her smile, her dimples, just her—I couldn't stop thinking about her. Kam. The way she hopped every three or four steps to keep up with me. The way she was always blowing her hair out of her face. The way she held her brother's hand when he was upset. The three freckles on her nose. And then there was the way she looked at me...

"I brought some wine," I said, holding up a bottle I'd picked up at the gas station. Nothing spectacular, but I couldn't show up empty-handed like *I need to have sex with you to get the love of my life out of my head.*

Maggie smiled. "Come on in." She stepped aside to let me through.

Her place was small but charming, even if it was a little feminine for my taste. Everything matched—her freaking tooth-brush matched her shower curtain—it was too much, but since it wasn't my place, it wasn't my problem. I'd been staying with her most nights for the past two weeks since Mom wouldn't let us have girls sleep over, at least not girls I was just hooking up with.

My relationship with Maggie was purely accidental. I mean, look: she was hot, she was nice, but she was too perfect, too girly, too…I don't know. I often felt like I wanted her to react more, even act crazy, just something to show me she had blood pumping through her veins. I guess you need kindness and an even temper-ament to be an elementary school teacher, but me…I needed fire.

Maggie got a couple of glasses from her tiny kitchen, and we sat down on her couch. I opened the bottle and poured her a glass and then one for me.

"To what do I owe this unexpected visit?" she asked.

"I just wanted to fuck you," I said, looking into her eyes.

How would she react to that? She squirmed; I could tell it made her uncomfortable. "Did anyone ever tell you how crude you can be sometimes?" she asked, taking a sip and looking at me with her sky-blue eyes.

"Yeah," I said, reaching out to stroke her arm. She was wearing pajama shorts with a matching silk tank top. Her skin was soft. "You like it, though, don't you?" I leaned closer, lifted her chin, and brought my mouth to hers.

She kissed me back but then pulled away and grabbed her glass of wine. "Are you in the mood for a movie?" she asked, standing up and walking over to find the remote control.

"Sure."

Halfway through, I don't even know which movie because I wasn't paying attention, in the darkness of the living room, her hand crept under the blanket she'd thrown across us and down into my pants.

She grabbed my dick. And I'm the kind of guy who doesn't need to be told twice. Five minutes later, she was kneeling before me, slowing sucking me off, while I had my hand in her hair. "Keep going," I said. I wanted to come in her mouth, but I knew she wouldn't let me. "Keep going. Deeper…" I murmured, closing my eyes and imagining it was someone else. I couldn't help it: in my mind, it was Kam, and just the thought of it aroused me in a way that Maggie never could. I was so hard, I only fit halfway in her mouth.

I came in her hand, and when I opened my eyes to see Maggie instead, I was so disappointed it put me in a bad mood. I wanted to get up and go, but I couldn't be an asshole. So I stripped her naked, buried my head between her legs, and began to pleasure her with my tongue.

She did come in my mouth.

Afterward, I helped her clear the wine glasses we'd left on the table, said goodbye, and went home, leaving the movie unfinished. Up in my room, I couldn't help but look out my window. I saw Kami. She had fallen asleep with the light on. I needed to touch her so damn badly… She would be at my house the very next day, and I had no idea what I'd do to avoid her. I wished I could just leave and get away from the temptation, but Mom had insisted Taylor could only have his party if I stayed there supervising and making sure nothing got out of control.

I looked out the window again. How had I managed to go from hating her so much to pining away for her?

Sometimes, I missed the hatred because it had helped me stay away from her. Without it, without the resentment, there was nothing holding me back. And damn…every day I was one step closer to the edge, to forgetting the reasons that kept me away from her.

On Saturday morning, I woke up in a cold sweat. As for my dreams, I won't say a word, but I'm sure you can guess who had the starring role. I was so horny, and I had an erection I couldn't get rid of, so I jumped in the shower before throwing on my tracksuit and heading out for a run.

I jogged all the way into town, ran along a few side streets, crossed the plaza, and stopped at Mill's. I wiped a bit of sweat off my face, hesitated, and then went inside. Of course, the fucking bell rang, and Kam turned right around and looked at me. I could see the words *good morning* forming on her lips with that false cheerfulness she had to show to the customers. That vanished, replaced by something much more authentic that she immediately tried to hide.

"Good morning, Mr. Di Bianco," she said, wiping her hands on her apron when I made it to the counter. "What will it be?"

"I'll take a coffee, Miss Hamilton," I said, feeling some of that pressure that had been building up inside me dying down. "Just a black coffee, thanks."

"For here or to go?"

To go, Thiago. To go. "I'll have it here," I replied, cursing myself.

I went to my usual table, and five minutes later, Kami walked over with a tray and a large white enamel cup.

"I brought you a slice of carrot cake," she added with a sweet smile. "On the house. I made it myself. It's not my best, but it's better than anything else you'll find around here."

Her modesty—or lack thereof—made me chuckle, but I accepted the cake with a nod. I looked around and noticed there was hardly anyone else there. "You feel like sitting down for a second?"

She thought it over briefly and then took a chair. "What are you doing up so early on a Saturday?" she asked.

You were in my head, I wanted to say, but instead I responded, "I don't know, I just had trouble sleeping." I stared down into my cup.

"You went out pretty late last night..."

"Are you spying on me, Kamila?" I asked, looking up at her. She blushed, and I couldn't help but grin.

"My desk faces your house. It's not hard to see what's going on there."

"Right." I didn't care. I liked that she was watching me.

"Where'd you go?" she asked.

Ugh. This was slippery terrain. I just stared at her, making it clear that I wouldn't answer that question.

"Not like I care," she continued, "I'm just asking because if you know a cool place to hang out at that hour in this sleepy town..."

How about my bedroom? I thought. *No, focus, Thiago.* "I feel like the kids at school are always throwing parties. Isn't that enough for you?" I took a sip of coffee and tried a bit of the cake. *Damn, that's good.*

"You like it?" she asked.

"It's dry," I lied, wanting to get under her skin.

"You wish. My cakes win prizes every year at the county fair."

"I guess the competition's not that stiff." I took another bite.

"You know, one day you could try just giving me a regular compliment without being mean."

"Fine," I said. "I've never seen anything as spectacular as you." I realized I should have thought about the consequences of my words a little longer. In the ensuing silence, she blinked, and her breathing sped up. I wished I could kiss her on the neck, just where I could see her jugular throbbing. I knew my words had excited her, and they were true: I'd never seen a more beautiful girl in my life.

"Now," I added, "was that compliment enough, or does the queen still need more?" I joked to break the tension.

Kam leaned back and grinned. "I'm not sure I'm the queen anymore," she said.

"That's right, they did knock you off your pedestal, didn't they?" Maybe I shouldn't have made light of it. It was messed up how everyone had Kam in their sights. They'd all admired her and loved her, and now they were watching with envy as someone tried to take her down.

"I prefer to say I've retired. I never wanted to be the center of attention," she said, tucking a strand of hair behind her ear.

I noticed the silver earring dangling from her earlobe and imagined sucking on it. Trying to ignore the image, I said, "Yeah, but that's what makes you deserve it. I've got to admit, though, it's funny watching you try to be a regular mortal."

"I don't know why you're trying to act like I've always been some kind of diva," she said, irritated. "I was just the head of the stupid cheerleading squad."

"Don't forget you were going out with the captain of the basketball team...and when he got the axe, you started going out with the new captain." That stung me again, thinking of her with my brother. "You're a cliché, you know that, right?"

Now red in the face, she asked, "Do you really think I'd go out with a guy just because he's captain of a stupid sports team I don't give a shit about?"

"Hey! Careful. Don't bad-mouth basketball, Kamila."

She rolled her eyes. "Anyway, I'm happy for Kate. I hope she enjoys it. Me, I'm doing exactly what I need to be doing right now."

Liar. "Yeah, you must love riding a bike to school and studying in whatever time you can find between serving people coffee so your grades don't suffer."

"If people only liked me because my family had money and I was the head cheerleader and I drove to school in an Audi convertible, then yes, I am happy that's all gone because it means whoever's left actually cares about the real me."

"Touché" I gulped down my coffee. "Either way, you're still the queen of Carsville High, much as I hate to admit it."

"Why would you hate to admit it?"

"Because the Kam I know, the Kam I like, is this one, not the stuck-up girl from the start of the school year." I got up and dropped a ten on the table. "I'll see you tonight to dig up our time capsule."

"You're actually coming?"

"I'm sorry to say I don't trust you two to dig a hole without falling in, so yeah, I'm coming."

"Are you going to dress up too?" Kam asked, shaking her head. "Wonders never cease, Mr. Di Bianco." Those two adorable dimples appeared in her cheeks.

"For sure. My costume is *dude who doesn't give a fuck about Halloween.*"

She laughed, and I forced myself to leave with the words, "See you around, Hamilton."

I felt worse than before I'd gone in. Why did I always want what I couldn't have?

CHAPTER SEVEN

Kami

WHEN I GOT OFF WORK, I WENT TO THE DI BIANCOS' TO HELP decorate for the party that night, to my mother's dismay. She wouldn't let my little brother come along, and he kicked and screamed, throwing a fit in a way that was completely unlike him. I couldn't do anything to convince her to let Cam help us decorate, and I could still hear him crying in his room when I left. I promised to bring him a bag of candy, but not even that calmed him down.

As Taylor and I began setting up, I asked, "Are you sure people are going to come?" After all, Aaron had been planning his party for weeks.

Cocking an eyebrow, Taylor said, "Don't insult me." He was wrapping a fake spiderweb around a tree. We put up lights, plastic skulls, plastic skeletons, giant plastic spiders, and lots of jack-o'-lanterns after almost three hours in the kitchen scooping out the seeds and carving spooky faces. Taylor's mother had helped us at first, but she'd gone upstairs to take a nap after a while because she had to work the late shift that night and she couldn't stand to witness what we were doing to her home. Taylor was determined to make the downstairs look like a haunted house.

"Don't you feel like you're overdoing it a bit?" I asked.

"Maybe I need to remind you, but Halloween is one of my favorite holidays."

"Is there a holiday you don't like?"

"Not really," he said, stopping what he was doing to give me a kiss. "What are you going to dress up as?"

"I don't know. You?"

Taylor grinned and said, "I've got a good costume planned— it's gonna scare the shit out of people. But it's a secret."

I loved the way he could still get excited like a little kid. He really wanted the party to be a success, and I knew he was doing it all for me, which was sweet. I would have felt uncomfortable and out of place at Aaron's party, and Taylor knew it. Here, though, I could just relax. "Is that your goal? To scare the shit out of people?" Of course, I knew it was.

"You know what my goal is," he said, coming up behind me and pushing me against the tree. "Finding dark corners where I can kiss you."

I smiled. "Now I know why you spent half an hour screwing in those red light bulbs all over the house," I responded.

"You know," he said, grinning and showing off his gorgeous teeth, "you're even smarter than you look."

He kissed me, cupping my face in his hands and thrusting his tongue deep into my mouth. I felt him get hard as he pressed his body against mine.

"I need to stop myself," he announced, pulling away just before he lost control.

"You sure?" I asked, tugging his T-shirt and going in for another kiss. I loved feeling his body against me, smelling his scent, that mix of masculine cologne and fresh pine…

His hands felt their way under my shirt and squeezed my breasts. "If you insist…" he said. I shivered and bit my lower lip, feeling overcome with desire. He pulled down my bra, and with his skin on mine, suddenly the cool outdoor air felt like a sweltering summer day. "Let's go to my room," he said, kissing me again.

I couldn't respond at first because he was smothering me in kisses. "We can't." I sighed.

"Why not?" He was panting against my neck, pressing his mouth against the most sensitive skin on my body. "God, I love it when you tremble like that."

I pushed him back as he started unbuttoning my jeans. "Tay, it's late already. If we're supposed to dig up our time capsule and have everything ready for when people arrive..."

"Shit. That's true," he said, but he couldn't keep his hands off me. "Why don't we just let Thiago dig up the time capsule and he can tell us what he finds."

I laughed and shoved him away.

"OK, I give up," he said, raising his hands in surrender.

I rearranged my clothes and took a step back. "See you later at the tree house," I told him with a quick kiss.

Back at my house, I found my brother waiting for me on the steps. I grinned at him and took a bag of candy I'd gotten at Tay's out of my back pocket, warning him not to tell Mom. He looked a little better now. I kissed him on the top of his head and went to my room.

So now I guess I had to come up with a stupid costume. I opened the box where I kept my Halloween stuff from previous years. God, some of these costumes were terrible. My friends had this thing that we should all wear matching outfits. I hated that, it was so unoriginal, but I'd always gone along with it. There was the bloody nurse costume, the wicked angel, the witch, the Bride of Chucky, the cowgirl... No way I was reusing any of those. What would they all be dressed as tonight? I wondered. Killer maids? Playboy bunnies? I thought about copying Thiago and dressing up as myself, but that would probably just attract more attention.

I looked back at my bed and saw my winter cheerleading outfit folded on the chair. It had come in the mail the day before—I guess whoever sent them out hadn't known I was off the squad. I'd had to pay for it, and now I wasn't even going to wear it. But I could, for one night…

I went to my brother's room and found him with chocolate all over his face and half the bag of candy gone.

"Cameron! You were supposed to eat just a few!"

He looked at me with no regret whatsoever in his eyes. "I'm in first grade. I don't know how to do division yet," he said. That was the kind of nerdy joke he found hilarious.

"Here's a simple problem for you," I told him. "One bag of candy equals one full stomach equals one pissed-off Mom when you don't eat your dinner. But it's out of my hands now. Do you have any of that fake blood left?"

Cam sat up. "What are you going to do with it?"

"I need to add a touch of horror to my costume."

"Let me help!" he shouted, jumping out of bed and momentarily forgetting about the rest of the candy. He pulled the fake blood from a box hidden at the back of his closet. God knows what all he was hiding in there.

I laid out my cheerleading uniform on an old sheet on the floor, and my brother and I both looked at it. "Should I feel bad about this?" I asked.

"Let's ruin it!" Cam shouted. I laughed, and we went at it with the blood and a pair of scissors until it looked like the uniform of a cheerleading zombie. I made a long gash across the belly like a machete wound and some holes in the skirt. When we were done, it looked positively horrifying. It was strange to think this was the fate of the last cheerleader uniform I'd ever own.

"You should cover your face in blood too," my brother said, and I told him I'd think about it. Was it a metaphor for what being a cheerleader had meant these last few years, and how glad I was to leave that all behind? Yes, it certainly was fitting.

I left my brother in his room and went to get ready, braiding my hair into pigtails and watching a YouTube Halloween makeup tutorial. I put dark shadows under my eyes and black lipstick on my lips. Where was I going to use black lipstick anyway? I'd probably bought it to shock my mom and then regretted it or just didn't want to put up with another of her lectures about the kind of makeup a respectable young lady should wear.

I didn't end up covering my face in fake blood. It smelled gross, so I just dabbed a little on my cheek. Once I was finished, I had to admit I didn't look too scary, but that wasn't the point. I was trying to tell people something: one, that there was no way I'd ever rejoin the squad; two, that I hated always having to dress up like my friends; three, that the scariest thing would be returning to my old life, surrounded by people who weren't actually my friends. I knew Kate would freak out. For her, that stupid cheerleading uniform was sacred. Looking at myself in the mirror, that only made me like it even more.

———

I found Dad in the hallway when I walked out, and when I saw his eyes widen, I couldn't help but chuckle.

"You look…" he evidently didn't know how to finish.

"Horrifyingly beautiful?"

"Yeah, that's exactly what I was going to say." He kissed me on the forehead and stopped to look at me another moment.

"What's up?" I asked.

His smile faded, and he sighed. "I'm leaving tomorrow, honey." I could see it was breaking his heart to have to put it into words.

"So soon? But…"

"We're signing the divorce papers next week. We all might as well get used to the idea that I can't live with you anymore."

"Where are you going to live?" I asked, trying to keep him from noticing that I was about to cry. I didn't want to make it any harder on him than it already was.

"I've got a job offer in Chicago. It's not what I had here, but I'm not in a position to choose right now."

"Chicago! It's so far." I felt a pain in my chest. We barely ever saw him now with all his work trips and his late hours. When was he going to find time to come see us from Chicago?

"Honey, it's just to stem the bleeding. I'll keep looking for something closer to home. But there's only so much work a financial adviser can do in a small town, and I need money if I'm going to untangle the situation I'm in. I promise I'll come see you whenever I can."

I looked at my shoes and tried to control my emotions. "I don't even have a car to drive there."

"Kami, I'll come visit as soon as I can." He forced himself to smile. "Now go to your party. I saw the Di Bianco place on my way in. It looks incredible. Go have a good time. We'll eat breakfast together before I leave tomorrow. Sound good?"

I nodded just as my mother emerged from my brother's room. Was she telling him Dad was going, and that we had no idea when we'd see him again?

"Did you give Cameron all that candy?" she asked. She was angry, but so what—she always was.

"Yeah," I replied, defiant.

"Don't you use that tone with me."

"Kamila was on her way out. She's got a party to go to," my father said, trying to stop us before we started fighting.

"And I guess you're just going to say nothing, huh? You think it's just hunky-dory for her to be going out with Taylor Di Bianco?"

Dad gave her an icy stare. "Unlike you, she hasn't kept any secrets from me." His coldness surprised even me.

Mom took a step back and then composed herself. "Do *not* be home later than two," she said.

I looked at Dad, who contradicted her: "You can stay out till four, honey." Turning to my mother, he continued, "It's literally next door, Anne."

Mom pursed her lips but didn't respond, instead turning around and going to her room.

"Thanks, Dad." I kissed him on the cheek, but there was a knot in my chest as I walked downstairs, and it felt hard to breathe.

As I went outside, even the bright lights in the Di Biancos' yard didn't cheer me up. It was almost dark, and I figured we had an hour before people started showing up. I checked my Instagram: Taylor had just posted his ninth or tenth story showing off his decorations, the food, the yard. Everyone would show up. I knew it.

I turned on my flashlight app and walked into the woods behind our houses. I was scared, walking out there alone, but that was where we said we were meeting, and I didn't want the brothers to think I was a coward. When I reached the tree house, I couldn't hear a thing, just the whistling of the wind and the scurrying of tiny animals. I heard a branch snap behind me and I turned around, aiming the flashlight. "Taylor?" I called. Another noise, and I turned in the other direction. "Taylor, this isn't funny." My hair was standing on end. I was so scared; I didn't know if I'd be able to summon the strength to run if I had to.

Something or someone touched my shoulder, and I spun around, raising my fists the way Dad had taught me to do so long ago. There was Thiago, who quickly dodged my punch and laughed at my clumsiness.

"Are you stupid?" I shouted, punching his arm. "You scared the shit out of me."

"Did I now?"

I put my hand on my heart, which was pounding out of my chest.

"Your costume is hilarious," he said. "Scary cheerleader...is that a thing?"

"It is now." I scowled.

"What are you going to do, kill people with your pom-poms?"

"How about you fuck off?" I said, turning around and walking to where I thought we'd buried the time capsule.

"Wrong way, Kamila," he said, taking me by the elbow and dragging me in the opposite direction.

"How do you know?"

"Because I do," he said, letting me go and striding off.

"Wait!" I said, trying to catch up. Three of his steps were like five of mine. "Shouldn't we wait for Taylor?"

"He knows how to get here."

"But..."

"Listen, you can stay back there and wait for him if you want." He gave me a wry smile, and I knew he was getting a kick out of seeing me so scared. I didn't stay and wait for Taylor, instead I stuck close to Thiago, trying to conceal the fact that I no longer found the plan so funny. We walked deeper into the woods, and I saw him hesitate for an instant, then count on his fingers. Had we really done all this just to bury a dumb time capsule? At last, he stopped in front of a twisted old tree.

"How do you know it was here?" I asked.

"Because I was the one who decided where to bury it, remember?"

The truth was, no, I didn't remember. "If it is, then right here I should be able to see..." I began, flashing my light on the tree.

"No, it's over here," Thiago said and walked around to the other side. And it was true. The spot was much lower than I remembered, but there they were, our initials. I smiled as I remembered carving them.

"Those are some good memories, huh?" I said.

"Yeah. Beautiful." His tone was indifferent. So much for my emotional reverie. "We need to start digging before it gets too late."

"What about Taylor?"

"He'll be here soon."

Thiago tossed me a shovel. We had been digging a minute or so when we heard footsteps. As I aimed the flashlight to greet Taylor, I got the fright of my life. I automatically dropped my shovel, hearing it land on the ground with a loud thump, and held up my hands to feign innocence. "We... We didn't..."

Then the loudest cackle in all of history rang out, and I pointed the beam of light into the face of the person laughing at me. "Are you fucking serious?" I screamed. "You nearly gave me a heart attack!"

"That was the idea, gorgeous!"

Thiago started laughing uncontrollably too. Taylor threw an arm around me and said to his brother, "I told you I had a killer costume."

"A cop?" I said. "Whatever. It does look realistic, though."

"Damn right it does. It's real," Taylor explained, picking up a shovel and sinking it into the dirt.

"Where'd you get it?" I asked, grabbing my own shovel in an attempt to help out.

"I've got my contacts," he said with an impish grin. "I'm gonna have a great time pretending to bust my party tonight."

I didn't doubt that. There was nothing that would scare a teenager more than seeing a policeman at a party where at least four state laws were being broken.

We kept digging—or rather, they did, because I got tired after about five minutes, so I just went through the motions. Soon Thiago struck something hard.

"I think this is it," he said, crouching down and pushing the dirt aside with his hands. He uncovered the metal box, and my nerves got the better of me. I knelt too, as did Tay, and we all struggled to pull it out.

"Damn, that's heavy," Taylor grunted, exhaling a lungful of air. We stared at it for a few seconds until he said, "We should open it, right?" He was now rubbing his hands together and breathing on them to warm them up. It must have dropped another ten degrees since we were setting up at his house.

"Yeah, unless you want to catch a case of pneumonia," Thiago responded.

Taylor did the honors, wiping off the last bits of dirt and lifting the latch. "Thiago, look! Our Captain America comics!" he shouted, grabbing one and flipping through the pages.

"I totally forgot we had put those in there," Thiago said.

I saw one of my old treasures. "Polly Pocket!" I called out, grabbing the little flower-shaped box and opening it to reveal the tiny house inside. I had spent hours playing with those as a kid. "And my Furby! Remember Furbies?"

"I hated those fucking things. I can still remember how it would wake me up in the middle of the night asking for food," Taylor said, putting aside his comics. There was all kinds of stuff inside: toys, drawings, coins. "Oh, shit, fifty bucks!" Taylor announced. "Why would we have left money in here?"

"It was in case we were starving in the future," Thiago remembered, and we all laughed.

"And there are our letters!" I said, grabbing the three envelopes with our names on them. Thiago looked weirdly serious as I asked, "Should we read them out loud? I can't remember what I wrote."

"Yeah," Taylor agreed, "let's do it!" He unwrapped a chocolate that was in there. I wasn't sure that was the best idea, and I asked if he really intended to eat it.

"Of course! Chocolate from the past, awesome!"

I shook my head in disgust and told him, "It's gonna make you sick. It must have expired years ago." But he shoved four more in his mouth before finally admitting, "Yeah, they do taste kind of weird."

"You really are a moron," Thiago said.

"Kami, read your letter," Taylor said, ignoring him.

I smiled nervously and began:

"*Dear future Kami: I hope that now that you're all grown up, you've learned to understand all the stuff that ten-year-old Kami still doesn't get. Like where do babies come from—*"

"I can explain all that to you," Taylor interrupted me, and I told him to shut up.

"*I hope you got into Yale. You know you want to be a veterinarian or a famous painter. You've got time to figure it out.* Damn. I completely forgot I wanted to be a vet."

"You don't remember how you used to pick up little animals on the roadside and from the woods?" Thiago asked. "You even brought us a bat one time." He and his brother looked at each other, reminiscing.

"It was a phase, all right? Now let me finish: *Tell Thiago that you're an adult now and you don't need his help anymore. And tell Taylor you'll always be his best friend. Tell him you love him like the big brother you never had and that you hope he'll finally let you use his chemistry set.* Yeah, can I use your chemistry set?"

"You can use whatever you like, babe," Taylor said with a nudge. "Just leave out that shit about loving me like a brother. I'm not into incest."

I knew I was blushing, and I was glad it was too dark out for either of them to see my face. I went on: "*Remember that no matter what happens, you and Tay and Thiago swore to be best friends forever. It's true that Thiago acts like a dummy a lot of the time, but you know he cares about you by the way he waits by his window every night to say good night using the flashlight signals you made up together.*"

Taylor cut me off: "Excuse me, what's this about the flashlights?"

"We had like a code, you know, because we could see each other through the window," I said with a shrug. It got quiet, so I hurried to finish: "*I hope you're really happy. I love you. Love, Kami from the past.* Well, that was interesting." I folded up the letter and stuck it in my pocket.

"Absolutely," Taylor said. "I'm up." He laughed as soon as he opened the envelope: "*Dear Taylor from the future. I hope you're playing for the NBA. If not, then go to hell. Take it easy. Taylor from the past.*"

"That's it?" I asked, unable to believe it.

"I guess I was dead set on it."

Thiago shook his head as Taylor and I looked at him. "Your turn, bro," Taylor said.

But Thiago hesitated. "I don't know if going into my past thoughts and feelings is the best idea."

"Come on!" I said. "It's fun!"

"Yeah, bro, do it!"

"No thanks," Thiago declined, and reaching into the box he brought out a magnifying glass, and said, "What is this doing in there?"

"I figured since you were the oldest, you'd probably have trouble seeing," Tay said with a laugh. "Now don't change the subject. Read it," Taylor exclaimed.

When Thiago insisted that he wouldn't, his younger brother tore it out of his hand. Thiago looked uncomfortable. I glanced back and forth between them, wondering what the big deal was, as Taylor started to read:

"*Dear future Thiago: I hope when you finally find this, you've stopped feeling the way you do. I hope Dad's stopped cheating on Mom and everything's gone back to the way it was before.*" Taylor stopped and looked at his brother. After a brief pause, he continued: "*I hope Tay still doesn't know about any of that, and I hope you're in college now playing for the best basketball team you can find. You're good, now get out there and live my dream. And another thing: I hope by the time you dig up this box, you've got the courage to tell Kam how you feel about her.*"

Fuck. I didn't see that coming. Taylor paused for a second and gripped the letter more tightly. I looked at Thiago, my heart racing.

"*Our kiss was even better than I'd thought it would be, and I'm sure she liked it too. She's the girl of my dreams, treat her right and tell her every day how special she is. See you in ten years. Thiago.*"

After he'd finished, Taylor asked, "You guys kissed?" He hadn't taken his eyes off the letter.

Thiago stood. "That was ages ago, dude."

Taylor stood up too. "Were you ever going to tell me?" he asked angrily.

I was speechless, and Thiago answered for me calmly. "Why would she? It was kiddie shit."

"What else did y'all do?"

"Nothing, Taylor," I said, but all I could think about was what had happened between us just a couple of weeks ago, or what had almost happened on the day Thiago came to talk to me about my brother.

"You were in love with her?" Taylor shouted.

I couldn't believe how closed-minded he was being. "Taylor, he was twelve years old."

"Who cares? I've been in love with you since I was nine."

I felt lightheaded. That was news. I took a step toward him, he looked so upset I just wanted to give him a hug, but he held out a hand to stop me. "The party's about to start. I'll see you there. I need some time to myself right now."

He turned around and walked off, and I watched him disappear into the trees.

"Did you know?" I asked Thiago.

"That he was nuts about you? Kam, who isn't?"

I didn't really know what that meant. Thiago crouched down and put everything back in the box, then turned on the flashlight on his phone and started walking back. "Come on," he said. "Leave your shovel, I'll come back and get them tomorrow."

I didn't say a word on the way back, and once we emerged from the woods into his yard, I could hear the music blasting from the Di Biancos' house.

"Let the party begin."

CHAPTER EIGHT

Kami

PEOPLE SHOWED UP EARLY. BY THE TIME I WALKED IN, TEN PEOPLE were in the living room, chattering with Taylor, who seemed to be enjoying himself. I hadn't caught sight of the angry cheerleaders, but I knew they'd turn up. Practically the whole basketball team was there, and I knew wherever the boys were, the cheerleaders wouldn't be far behind—even if Aaron had announced his party first.

Thiago nodded at a few people, and as soon as he could, he made a beeline upstairs to his room. Or so I assumed. Nobody was talking to me, and I wasn't sure whether Ellie would even come. I started to feel slightly uncomfortable when it dawned on me I might not have anyone to talk to. Taylor was all but ignoring me, drinking beer and laughing. He seemed to want to prove he didn't need me to have fun. Was he really that angry?

I walked over to the table where we'd set out potato chips and sandwiches earlier. There was also a big bowl of punch, Taylor's specialty, which he'd spiked with enough booze to kill a rhino. I don't know how many types of alcohol he'd put into that repugnant mixture, but I got a glass and filled it up, telling myself I wouldn't let anyone ruin my night. My father was leaving the next day, the whole school seemed to hate me, my boyfriend was mad at me, and I was worried I was in love with Thiago. Hearing his letter had made it worse, though at the same time it had revealed so much to me.

I downed my first glass within five minutes and felt my whole body warm up. I looked around, and there seemed to be twice as many people now. Most of them were wearing costumes they'd already worn before, but a few of them had put some time into dressing up and they looked really scary, like Harry Lionel in his incredible Khal Drogo costume.

"I've got to admit, your costume is fucking original. Are you trying to say something with it?" I heard someone whisper in my ear.

"Jesus!" I said, whipping around. "You scared the hell out of me, Julian." He was dressed as a clown. I hated clowns.

"That's the idea," he said, pouring himself a glass of punch and grimacing as he drank it. "Who's trying to kill us?"

"Taylor," I said, looking over to where he was talking to a group of freshmen girls.

"Trouble in paradise?" He tried his punch again. "You know, this shit is really disgusting."

"We just had a silly argument," I said, feeling a stab of jealousy to see Taylor laughing and having such a good time with them.

"And what about the elder Di Bianco brother?"

I shrugged. "I don't know if I care. To be honest, I'm tired of the drama. I want to have fun tonight. Every day, it seems like more and more bullshit comes my way, and I'm honestly not about to let some stupid letter ruin my night." I refilled my glass and forced myself to drink, pinching my nose so I wouldn't taste it.

"Letter?" Julian asked, clapping me softly on the back when the liquor made me cough.

"Don't worry about it," I responded. "You feel like dancing?"

He hesitated. "I'm not really the best dancer…"

"Just stand next to me and jump up and down," I said, dragging him to the middle of the room. A makeshift dance floor had evolved, and I started dancing and jumping around.

He watched me, smiling, but there was something creepy about him. I guess it was his costume, but a shiver ran down my spine. I kept dancing and turned to look the other way, trying to have fun while ignoring all the looks I knew I was drawing. I managed to enjoy myself until I saw Kate walk through the door.

Just as I'd expected, the other cheerleaders, all my former friends, walked in behind her in exactly the same outfits: bodysuits with bones painted on them. I guess they were supposed to be skeletons, but it was obviously just an excuse for a sexy getup. Kate frowned when she saw me.

"Looks like the dead sisters' club has arrived," Julian said.

Ellie wasn't with them, so I walked off to look for her, finally finding her in the kitchen, sitting on the counter. She was dressed as Katniss from *The Hunger Games*. She looked stunning, and I was glad she hadn't played along with the rest of the cheerleaders, but I wasn't surprised, either: she'd never been one to show off her body. One thing was weird, though: she was talking to Danny.

I hung back for a second in the doorway until she looked up at me. She tensed, and Danny noticed, and then he saw me too. I walked in slowly with Julian at my side.

"I've been looking for you," I said, trying to pretend my ex-boyfriend wasn't there.

"Yeah, I just got here, and came right in to grab a drink," she said, trying to pretend like she hadn't been flirting with my abusive ex-boyfriend. Or had I just imagined it?

"Nice costume," Danny said, looking me up and down.

He was dressed as a soldier, fake machine gun and all. As he lifted it and pointed it at Julian, he said, "Sometimes I wish it were real."

"You think that's funny?" I asked.

"No. I'd actually like to shoot you all dead." I froze. Then a second later, he said, "God, I'm kidding. I guess your sense of humor disappeared along with everything else everyone used to like about you."

I ignored him and asked Ellie if she'd come to the living room with me. "Can't you hear? It's our song! Let's go dance before they switch to hip-hop," I said, trying to act normal.

"Hell yeah!" she said, grabbing my hand and pulling me away. Julian was right on our heels. By now, the whole house was packed. I guess Taylor really had the whole school eating out of the palm of his hand. I looked around for him, but he was nowhere to be seen. The music was booming, and I was ready to dance, but instead Ellie dragged me over to the drinks table.

"You want one?" she shouted.

"Why not?"

She poured a cup of punch for herself, one for me, and one for Julian, and we toasted. I asked Ellie about Danny.

"He came over to talk to me. Honestly, it was kind of weird, his trying to hook up with me, but he's probably just doing it to piss you off."

"Ellie, do you like him?" I asked, praying the answer would be no.

"Of course not! I'd never do that to you, Kami. You know the rule: Friends' exes are off limits."

In my heart, though, I knew she was lying. "Ellie, I'm only telling you this to keep you safe: Danny's a bad guy." I had been blind when I'd dated him, but eventually I started to understand, and I regretted ever letting him manipulate me. He was a violent, abusive narcissist.

"Can we not talk about Danny?" she asked. "Let's talk about your boyfriend instead. You know he got me with that fucking costume of his. I thought I was screwed. Who the hell dresses as a cop at a party full of teenagers?"

"I guess that's what makes it funny," I said. I wanted to be sure she understood what I meant about Danny, but I knew it would get me nowhere. At least not tonight. So I asked her if she had seen Tay, who by now I had to assume was deliberately ignoring me.

"He's over there," she said, pointing to the couch by the window, surrounded by his friends and all the cheerleaders.

"I'll be right back," I said, setting my drink down and walking over. When I reached him, he was lighting a cigarette. I stopped in front of him, as if the other people there didn't exist, and asked, "Can we talk?"

"I'm busy," he replied.

"Taylor…"

"What the fuck do you want, Kami? You kissed my brother and didn't tell me."

"Yeah, when I was a fucking kid!"

"I don't care. You should have told me. Fuck, he should have mentioned it too."

"Why, Taylor? Thiago and I have just barely started getting along and—"

"And why is that?" he interrupted me, standing up and walking away from the curious onlookers. He took my arm and pulled me to a corner. "Why is it all of a sudden you two are so chummy?"

I couldn't think of a response, and he went on.

"Don't try to tell me that my brother, who's hated you for years, who's basically stopped talking to me since we got to this town, and who obviously can't stand the fact that I'm going out with you, has all of a sudden just decided that you're the greatest?"

"I…"

"What happened between you, Kami? I saw you get out of his car the day of the storm. What happened to make you two like each other again?"

I nearly started shaking as I remembered how we'd kissed in the car. Just thinking of it again made my palms sweat.

"We talked," I said, hoping he wouldn't hear the trembling in my voice.

"You talked?" He narrowed his eyes.

"Yeah, we talked."

"About what?"

"Like…I don't know, Taylor. We talked about what happened that day. I said I was sorry, he said he was sorry. I think we both had repressed a lot of stuff we needed to let out."

"I don't like how he looks at you."

Fuck. Fuckfuckfuck.

"What do you mean?"

"Well, the same way I look at you. And don't try to tell me otherwise."

As I tried to think of a response, someone came up behind me and put their arms around my shoulders. It was Julian again. "You guys are so lame. Could you stop fighting for once and try to enjoy yourselves?"

Taylor shifted his eyes away from mine to look at Julian. "Do you mind? I'm trying to talk to my girlfriend."

Julian pulled me toward him and said, "Oh, she's your girlfriend? Sorry, I didn't know, since you've spent the whole fucking party ignoring her."

"Julian, don't get involved," I said, trying to shrug him off.

Taylor got in his face. "Who the fuck are you?" he shouted. "Her fucking babysitter?"

"I'm her friend, and I don't like seeing people ignore her."

With an acid grin, Taylor turned to me. "So it's not just my brother. You've got other guys after you too?"

Before I could respond, Julian said, "Oh shit, he knows about Thiago?"

Furious, Taylor looked at me and shouted, "What the fuck do I need to know about Thiago?"

"Nothing!" I couldn't believe this was happening. "And Julian, can you shut up? You're only making this worse."

"I'm just trying to defend you!" he said.

"I don't need anyone to defend me!" *Was everybody at this damn party out of their minds?*

"You could fool me," Julian responded.

"To hell with this shit," Taylor said, "I'm out of here." He walked past us and vanished into the people dancing in the living room. I tried to follow him, but Julian grabbed my arm and held it tight.

"Kam, stop letting people string you along."

Trying to break free, I pleaded, "Why don't you stop telling me what to do?"

"You look pathetic."

By now, I was furious. "Do you hear yourself?" I asked him. "You're supposed to be my friend!"

"I am? That's news, because I care about you, but you sure don't seem to care about me! Friendship is a two-way street, you know."

He was right. I had been so focused on my own problems I'd almost forgotten the rest of the world existed. "I'm sorry, Julian," I said. "You're right. I'm just having a tough time right now, and..."

"Honey, I know." He pulled me into a hug, a little too close, a little too tight. But it was Julian, he was gay, he couldn't have feelings for me. Could he?

"And I'm here for you."

I took a step back once he let his arms slacken. "I appreciate that, Julian, but just let me come to you instead of trying to solve my problems for me."

"Kam, you need help. I'm the only friend you have left."

Was that true? I looked at all the people dancing and sweating. Everyone was with someone. Everyone was having a blast. Then there was me. I looked around for Ellie. There she was again. With Danny. *What the hell was going on?* "I appreciate the offer, but I'm fine," I said and walked off.

I got another glass of punch, but my stomach told me I'd better lay off. I looked for Taylor, but he had vanished, and so had Ellie, and I didn't want to think about what she might be doing. As for Julian, I don't know. He was just rubbing me the wrong way.

I didn't fit in there. I knew that now. Not that I hadn't suspected it before, but that sudden sensation of being totally out of place was painful, especially since my boyfriend had supposedly organized the party for me. People were staring at me, I could tell. And they enjoyed seeing me squirm, watching how no one came to my rescue.

On the other side of the room, Kate took a drink and whispered something to Marissa, who glared at me and laughed. I turned, ready to walk out the front door and go home, but then I saw them.

Danny and Ellie.

Kissing.

Kissing passionately by the column next to the door. Ellie's hands were wrapped around his neck, and he had his hands under her shirt.

I felt like I was drowning. So I turned back, grabbed a bottle, and walked upstairs. I was desperate to get away from those people. I couldn't handle feeling their eyes on me, being reminded over and over how they had all betrayed me or ignored me. Once upstairs, the memories overwhelmed me. I saw the door to Lucy's room, and I wanted to break down and cry. I went to Taylor's door, directly across from Thiago's, and knocked. I opened the door; the room was empty but just then the door across the hall flew open.

"Hey, nobody can fucking be up here!" Thiago shouted in exasperation, but when he saw it was just me his anger faded. Had he been sleeping? How could he with all that racket downstairs?

I noticed he wasn't wearing a shirt, and his Adidas track pants hung low on his hips, revealing his sculpted abs and obliques. *God, he's ripped*, I thought, tearing my eyes away. When I looked up, I saw the surprised look in his green eyes. "If you're looking for my brother," he said, "he's out in the yard acting like a jerkoff."

I hadn't even considered going outside in the freezing cold. "I just wanted to be alone for a minute," I said.

"You OK?"

"Yeah, great," I replied, stumbling. That punch was really strong.

"Great and drunk, I see. How much have you had?"

"Dunno."

"Why'd you leave the party?"

"No one wants me there. I'm an outcast now."

"Kamila, you're anything but."

"How come you don't call me Kam anymore?"

"I do sometimes."

"You used to do it always."

"Back then you didn't piss me off the way you do now," he said.

"Why would you be pissed at me now?"

"Have you seen yourself?"

"Every day in the mirror, why?"

"You're wasted."

I stepped toward him and tripped over my own feet; he reached out to catch me.

"I just had a couple glasses of punch," I said.

"One glass of that poison is enough for a whole night."

As he pulled me up, I felt my stomach churning, and I brought my hand to my mouth to keep myself from vomiting.

"Kamila, for fuck's sake," he said, pulling me directly into his bathroom. I managed to fall on my knees and lift the toilet lid just before I started vomiting. It was like the girl in *The Exorcist*.

"I'm going to kill Taylor," Thiago muttered, holding my hair back until I'd gotten the last drop of alcohol out of my body.

CHAPTER NINE

Thiago

I GRABBED MY PHONE AND LOOKED AT MY MESSAGES. MAGGIE wanted to meet for dinner the next day.

I can't, I typed brusquely and hit send as Kam walked out of the bathroom looking lost and exhausted. It made me want to tuck her into my bed with me, and rub her back until she closed her eyes and fell asleep. But instead, I said, "The door's over there," annoyed by my own thoughts. It was bad enough, Taylor knowing I'd had a thing for Kam when we were little. I couldn't believe I'd forgotten that stupid letter. Not until it was actually in my hands did I remember what it had said.

"Can I just stay here awhile?" she asked. And I was concerned by what I saw in her. Not just weariness, not just drunkenness, but a sadness that made me wish I could hug her. I wanted to punch whoever had made her feel that way.

"Shouldn't you go to Taylor's room?" I asked, watching her walk around to the other side of the bed and collapse there. She was the same Kam as always, doing whatever she wanted, not caring about the consequences, not caring if she'd overstepped a line.

"Taylor hates me," she said, folding her hands as if in prayer and tucking them under her left cheek. It was all I could do not to wrap my arms around her.

"He'll get over it." I said to calm her down, but part of me knew it was a lie. The fact that we had kissed as kids wasn't going to sit well with my brother. We had squabbled over Kamila when we were younger. He'd get mad that I picked on her; I'd get jealous about that special something they shared.

"It's not just him. Everyone hates me," she said.

"No one hates you."

"Yes, they do. I don't know why, but it's like I've got a contagious disease all of a sudden. And I don't care, I swear I don't. I was tired of having to keep up that image. But my friends just turning their backs on me..."

"If they turned their backs on you, they're not your friends."

She looked up at me, and I felt a throbbing in my groin. How did she do it? Those eyes, those lips... I couldn't take it.

"I'm a bad person," she confessed. And whatever heat I was feeling turned cold.

"Kam, what the fuck are you talking about?"

"What we did in your car...what I tried to do a few days ago..."

I ran it all through my head. Her standing before me, pulling me in and trying to kiss me. The throbbing sensation came back, and I was dying to take her right there. I looked at the ceiling to try to control myself. "You screwed up. Anyone can screw up."

"If you were with me and I did that with your brother, would you still see it that way?"

"If you were with me, you'd never feel tempted to do something like that with anyone else," I said without thinking. I didn't want to think like that—Kami wanting me more than she did Taylor—because it probably wasn't true. He was better for her, a better person, more fun, more attentive...more everything.

I felt her roll over until her body was right up against mine.

"Have you ever imagined being with me?"

I closed my eyes. Of course I had. Ever since our first kiss those thoughts had never stopped running through my head, not even after I grew up and started dating. Not even once I had a girlfriend. Kam had always been there. It was almost scary to me, the way I'd never been able to get her out of my mind.

"No," I said.

She fell back on the pillow. Now we were both staring at the ceiling.

"I should go," she said, sitting up. I couldn't keep myself from grabbing her arm and holding her back.

"Of course I've imagined it, Kamila," I admitted once our eyes had locked and she'd decided to stay there, torturing me like no one ever had before. Longing for something I couldn't have was painful.

"So what's it like, in your head?" She asked so gently it threw me off.

"I imagine us in this room."

She gulped, and I wanted to run my tongue along her neck, feel her heart rate quicken. I wanted to slide my hand under her skirt and touch her until she was desperately screaming my name.

"Why here?" Her voice was low.

"Because we do it over and over, I never give you a break. I make love to you until you can't anymore, and then, once you catch your breath, we go at it again."

Stop, Thiago, an inner voice was telling me.

"Why are you telling me this?" she asked.

Because I want you more than anything in this world. "You wanted to know."

"I guess I shouldn't have asked." Her voice was soft as she looked away briefly. "Did I really mean so much to you way back when?"

It took me a second to understand that she was referring to the letter. "Kam, you still mean that much to me."

"I do?" She seemed surprised.

I pulled myself up and couldn't help but tuck a lock of blond hair behind her ear. She trembled even from such a simple touch, and I wished she were mine. "Did you really not know that?" I asked.

"You hated me just a few weeks ago."

"I can hate you and want you at the same time."

"Do you still hate me?" she asked, blinking in confusion.

Her lips were hardly an inch from my face, and the urge to kiss her was practically irresistible. "I'll hate you as long as I'm not the one to tell you good night, pick you up at your front door, kiss your lips, or touch you until you come..."

"Thiago, please." She put a hand over my mouth to keep me from talking.

"Kam, you better not touch me because if you do, we'll fuck things up." But it was too late, we couldn't stop. I held her wrist where it was and then ran the tip of my tongue gently over her delicate skin, scratching her with my stubble. I tugged her hand toward my mouth ever so slightly, kissing my way up her arm, past her elbow. We looked at each other for a few seconds, and it felt like hours had gone by, hours during which she was conflicted and I was trying not to let myself think about anything except her, there with me, in my bed. She slowly lay down next to me, and I took it as an invitation. My kisses continued up her sweet, tender neck, where I could feel the blood pumping in her veins beneath her caramel skin.

"Thiago..." she exhaled slowly.

"Let me touch you. Please," I begged. I would throw myself at her feet if I had to, I didn't care. "It'll stay between us. I promise."

She closed her eyes. That had to mean yes.

I moved on top of her, pressing the length of our bodies together. Then I buried my head in her neck, slowly covering her in kisses, like I'd been wanting to do ever since that time in my car. Eventually, when I reached her breasts, I bit her nipples through her costume.

"Did I mention to you how amazing you look in this stupid outfit?"

"What, you want me to cheer for you now?" she joked.

"Shh," I said, pulling up her shirt to kiss her belly button.

She grabbed my hand and started sucking my fingers. "I could suck something else if you like," she said.

I couldn't believe it. But when I looked up, I could see the lust in her eyes. She pushed me back, I stood up, and soon she was on her knees before me. I thought she was joking, but her hand was in my pants now and I couldn't turn back... She challenged me with her gaze, and I was happy to let her have her way. She was touching me, stroking me. I put my hand on top of hers and stroked myself too. She bit her lip and leaned in.

"Wait," I said. I needed to cherish this moment, needed to watch her wanting me. I knew I'd never get that image out of my head now, and I didn't care anymore. She opened her mouth, and I put it in. Was I dreaming? I closed my eyes and cursed aloud as her tongue passed over the tip just before she took me all the way in.

"Fuuuuck," I said, leaning my head back.

Then I opened my eyes. Nothing had ever turned me on so much. And I'd never get this image out of my head. We locked eyes, and I knew this would become another chapter in the book of Kam and Thiago. Our story had started long ago, but the question now was: Where would it go from here? Would there be a climax and a resolution? Or would it stay here, at the introduction?

I pushed her back and asked, "Where'd you learn to do that?"

Kam just smiled.

"Never mind," I said immediately regretting the question. "I'd rather not know."

I reached under her skirt and started touching her over her panties. Then I pushed the fabric aside, sliding my fingers in softly. She was wet, and my mouth started watering. She grabbed my wrist forcefully, and I couldn't tell if she wanted me to stop or didn't want to let me go. I slipped a finger in and out, and she moaned, and I could feel myself getting even harder. "You like that?" I asked.

"Mm-hm," she said.

And I leaned in and bit her lip. Her arms wrapped around me and pulled me close, and we kissed, our tongues intertwining in an erotic dance. Her mouth tasted like my toothpaste, and it turned me on even more to know she'd had the audacity to use my toothbrush.

She was tense, breathless, and I couldn't stop touching her. She stopped kissing me to bite down on my shoulder, almost spasming. I pulled back a bit to see if she was all right, but she said, "No, please, keep going" as the last waves of her climax shook through her.

My God... How many nights had I fantasized about this? Making her come, watching her orgasm in my arms. I guided her hand to my member. "Please, touch me," I said, and she did, and, just as our lips joined again, there was a knock at the door.

We both froze.

"Thiago, can I come in?" It was my brother's voice.

Her eyes widened, and she jumped off the bed. I looked at her and back at the door and whispered, "Get in the bathroom." No sooner than I'd said it, she vanished.

"I can't find Kami," Taylor said when I opened the door.

"Really?" I felt like a complete bastard.

"I don't know, man, maybe she went home," Taylor said, frustrated. "She's not picking up the phone, or texting me back."

He took out his phone again, and I had the sudden image of him hearing her phone buzz in the bathroom, so I stopped him and said, "Come on, I'll help you look for her," almost dragging him out of my room and closing the door behind me. But he was so worried I don't think he noticed my haste as we started down the stairs.

"I was a total jerk," he said. The music was louder than ever, and the party was really raging now.

"Why do you say that?"

"Your letter upset me, and I blamed her. You should have told me."

"I know," I shouted, hoping he could hear me over the music. Everyone turned to look when we appeared. I'd forgotten I didn't have a shirt on until the girls started catcalling and giggling.

"Thiago, for fuck's sake, put on some clothes," my brother murmured, still looking around for his girlfriend.

His girlfriend.

Kam was his girlfriend, and I had just been about to have sex with her in my bed.

"Sure, let me go grab a T-shirt."

As soon as I opened the bedroom door, I felt a gust of icy air on my chest, and my hair stood on end. My window was wide open, and it didn't take a genius to know where Kam had gone. I looked out in time to see her slipping through her front door.

Thiago, dammit.

You're playing with fire.

CHAPTER TEN

Kami

I ALMOST CRACKED MY HEAD OPEN WHEN I JUMPED OUT OF Thiago's window, but it didn't matter, I had to get out of that house. How could I have done that?

I could always blame the alcohol, say it hadn't been the real me because otherwise, how could I explain cheating on my boyfriend, and like *that*?

But it wasn't the first time Thiago and I had shared…something. And this was the farthest we'd taken it yet. That time in his car a few weeks ago had been an isolated incident, an attempt to heal past wounds or put a happy ending on a childhood romance, a way of learning not to hate each other so we could move on. The almost-kiss at school, that would never have happened if I hadn't been so upset about Cameron getting bullied. But this time…

I loved Taylor. I knew I did. But what I felt for Thiago was something different. Something forbidden. Something that drove me absolutely insane.

Stop it. Stop it, Kamila. Taylor's the one for you. Taylor's the one who takes care of you, who respects you, who makes you laugh, who supports you while everyone else at school despises you—he doesn't give a damn about showing how much you mean to him in front of them. Thiago's not even a student, he's a coach! He's your boyfriend's brother, and besides, he's too serious, too standoffish, too sarcastic. Taylor's the right choice. He always will be.

Taylor...

In my room, I plugged in my phone, which had gone dead, and opened my messages.

Taylor had called me like ten times.

Please, Kami, where are you?

Please, Kami, I'm worried.

Babe, come on, answer the phone. I'm sorry, OK?

I called back, and he picked up immediately.

"Where are you? Are you all right?"

I fell back in bed and closed my eyes.

"I'm fine," I said in a tired voice.

"Where are you?"

"I'm at home. I'm sorry. I just drank too much, and I started feeling bad."

"Listen, Kami, I'm sorry. I'm sorry I acted like that. It's just...I don't know, I have this feeling like something's going on between you and my brother. I don't know what it is or why you two are hiding it."

I was literally the worst person in the world. "Taylor, there's nothing going on between Thiago and me..." Why was I lying? Was I incapable of being honest with myself? It's because I loved them both. That's why.

"I know," he said after a pause. "I know, and that's why I'm sorry. You want me to come over? You want to come back here? Come sleep with me. Mom won't be back until noon tomorrow..."

It was tempting, and if the thing with Thiago hadn't happened just half an hour before, I'd have accepted his offer without hesitating. But I couldn't. I couldn't get into his bed after I'd just crawled out of his brother's. I couldn't let myself fall that low. "I'm tired. We should leave it for another day."

For a few seconds, he said nothing, but then he gave in. "Fine. Get some rest, OK? We can go for a walk tomorrow or have breakfast or something, if you want."

"We need to work on our human sexuality project."

"You're damn right we do," he said in that sly tone that always made me laugh.

"Tomorrow at the library, then?"

"Yeah. I'll drive."

"Sounds good," I said, trying to clear out that sadness in my chest so I could get on with my life.

"Good night, babe." He sighed.

"Good night."

We hung up, and I undressed and put on my pajamas. Before I got into bed, I couldn't help but look outside at the room across from mine. Thiago had drawn his curtains. He almost never did that, and I felt a twinge of guilt again. Was he feeling just as bad as me?

Of course he was. I mean, it was his brother we were talking about.

Shit...

I got into bed and tried to sleep.

The next morning, I woke up with a head-splitting hangover. Parts of my body ached that I didn't even know existed. My ears were ringing, I could hardly open my eyes, but before getting in the shower, I reached over and checked my Instagram.

My friends' stories started off with them drinking and taking selfies and smiling, and ended with them wasted—dancing, jumping on the Di Biancos' furniture, even hooking up while people filmed them.

I didn't realize what was happening until the notifications started flooding in from all my followers. I stopped looking at stories and went to my profile page. What I saw made me sit up in bed. I couldn't believe my eyes.

On my feed was a photo, posted from my own account, of Kate and me from years back, when we were twelve. Our arms were around each other and we were smiling, but there was a big red X over the top, and below it read *I HATE YOU, YOU WANNABE.*

What the...

The comments said: *YOU'RE THE WANNABE.*

YOU'RE A SHITTY FRIEND.

NOBODY LIKES YOU.

FAKE.

YOU SUCK.

Most of the comments were defending Kate, but some of them took my side too.

KATE'S A BITCH AND SHE DOESN'T DESERVE YOU.

YOU'LL ALWAYS BE QUEEN BEE.

Fuckfuckfuck.

Who had hacked my account? How? Where had they gotten that photo? And why were they trying to hurt me?

One comment especially caught my eye, from a user named @omv_ovamat, whose profile photo was an image of Momo. It was scary. I hated that stupid doll, and I wondered what the hell was going on. The user had written: *NOW YOU'RE LIKE ME, AND SOON YOU'LL BE MINE.*

The profile had zero followers and no posts, and I was the only account it followed.

What the hell? I won't lie, I was terrified, but I tried to keep in mind just how weird things had gotten at school too. Didn't people in Carsville have anything better to do? I erased the photo and tried to text Kate on WhatsApp to apologize, but she'd blocked me. It made sense, but still, did she really think I was capable of posting something like that? And who had hacked my account? I changed my password. I couldn't believe all this had happened, and it wasn't even 9 a.m.

I showered and went downstairs for breakfast. I was so wrapped up in my own troubles that I'd totally forgotten Dad was leaving. His suitcases were piled up by the door—that was all I could take. As soon as I saw him eating breakfast with my brother, the tears started to fall. Dad looked up from his cereal and walked over, enveloping me in a big hug.

"Oh, honey…"

He was one of those guys who just made you feel protected. And around him, I turned back into a little girl. A little girl who needed her dad and whose heart would break when she had to watch him go. "Dad, stay, please," I begged, even though I knew it was unfair.

"Don't cry," he said, stroking my hair with his giant hands. "I'll be back in a few weeks to see you guys."

Something inside me knew that wasn't true. With all the problems he'd been having, how would he find time for us? My brother didn't get up, and when I looked over at him, the grimace on his face made me realize I needed to get a hold of myself. *You can't let Cameron see you like this. You've got to be strong for him.* So I forced a smile, let Dad go, and wiped away the tears. "What's for breakfast?" I asked, trying and failing spectacularly to sound normal.

"Captain America cereal!" my dad said.

I tried to show enthusiasm. "Whoa, Captain America, cool, I want to try it!" I sat next to my brother, feeling better as the tears on my cheeks dried.

How awful it felt to think that was the last time my father would wake up there to have breakfast with us—we wouldn't see him coming home tired from work in the evenings, smiling, and pulling a chocolate bar out of his coat for us.

Divorce sucked.

"OK, guys, I really should go," he said after loading the dishwasher.

As he said that, we heard doors opening and closing upstairs, and a few minutes later, my mother came down in a pair of jeans and a white knit sweater, with knee-high boots and her blond hair pulled back like a ballerina's. She looked gorgeous.

"I'm headed out," my father said after glancing over at her.

"No need to rush," she responded, dropping her bag on the kitchen table. "You got everything you need for the trip?"

"Yeah, everything's ready," Dad said, walking over to my brother, who stood up on his chair and hugged him tight. Cameron burst into tears, and Dad whispered something into his ear, but it didn't seem to do much good, he just held on tighter. Dad carried him to the front door and set him down. I wouldn't cry again, I told myself. I needed to be strong for Dad, for Cameron...

"Love you, Dad," I said, wrapping my arms around him again.

"I love you too, princess," he said, kissing my forehead and turning to Mom. She picked up Cameron, and the look on her face was strange.

"Take care of yourself," Dad said, "and take care of them." He gave her a soft kiss on the cheek. I was surprised to see her eyes begin to water. Maybe she did have human feelings?

"Let..." she began, then paused. "Let Kamila know when you get there." I guess she realized she could no longer ask much more from him. Once my father walked out that door, their lives would separate, and they'd both have to start over from zero.

Dad went to his car, and, with tears in our eyes, the three of us watched him go. My brother was sobbing uncontrollably while

I managed to keep a grip. A single tear rolled down Mom's cheek, which she wiped away as soon as she felt it.

"Let's go inside, it's cold," she said, pulling Cam along with her.

I stayed in the doorway, watching Dad's car disappear and wondering when life, or karma, had decided to turn against me so sharply.

I had just enough time to splash some water on my face before my alarm went off. I had completely forgotten that Taylor and I had made plans to go to the library together. I told Mom I was headed out to study and walked outside to meet Taylor in front of his house. Imagine my surprise when I found not him there but Maggie. With Thiago.

"Hey, Kami," she said cheerfully before I could turn back without making a spectacle. Who the hell was she to call me Kami? Were we supposed to be friends or something? As far as I remembered, we hadn't parted on the best of terms after our little meeting to discuss how the other kids were beating up on my brother.

I forced a smile as I watched Thiago and his...girlfriend? Hearing my name, he froze, his expression half-surprised, half-frightened. I mean, shit, it hadn't even been twelve hours since I'd had his dick in my mouth. "Hey there, neighbor," he said distantly. I had to give it to him: he had a talent for acting like there was nothing going on. To make matters worse, he grabbed Maggie around the waist and kissed her so hard it turned my stomach. I thought I was going to vomit.

"Is Taylor home?" I asked, wishing I could sink into the ground and vanish.

Thiago scowled. "He's busy cleaning up all the shit his friends left behind after the party. Why, are you here to help him?"

Fuck. I'd forgotten all about that. "Yeah," I said abruptly. "Can I go in?"

"*Mi casa es tu casa*," he said, throwing an arm over Maggie's shoulders.

I walked straight past them, wishing I could shove him on the way. In the living room, I opened my eyes wide with horror. "Jeeeesus..."

I saw Taylor in the kitchen doorway with an enormous plastic bag. "Hey, love," he said, looking stressed.

"Taylor, this house is a wreck."

"My mom's going to kill me." He came over to give me a kiss.

"Can I help you?" I asked.

"I'd be deeply grateful."

We started picking up as Thiago came back in and plopped down on the sofa with Maggie. They put on a movie and started making out while we cleaned up. They couldn't keep their hands to themselves, touching each other as if we didn't even exist. Watching Thiago nibble her ear, kiss her neck, stick his tongue in her mouth, and glance over at me to see if I was watching... I couldn't handle it.

"You know, you *could* help us out," I hissed, frowning at him until he pulled away from his girlfriend.

"Excuse me?" he said, and in a perverse way, I could tell he was enjoying this. "I could do what now?" He raised his hand to his ear as if he were hard of hearing.

"You were at the party too."

"No, dear. I was in the house where the party took place. That's totally different."

"You were drinking," I added. I couldn't stop myself. I didn't care if I was right or wrong, I just couldn't stand seeing him with her. Not after what we had done the night before. Not after that orgasm, after him touching me, him kissing me...

"Yeah, I drank one beer, in my own home, at a party I didn't organize. So no, I don't plan on lifting a finger, get it?"

"You're a jerk," I murmured, turning around and continuing sweeping.

"I'm a what?" he said, getting up and walking toward me.

"You heard me, jerk."

We faced each other, both clenching our teeth, until he finally thought better of it.

"Taylor, someone here seems to need you!" he shouted. Then he asked me in a voice so soft no one else could hear it, "Something bothering you, little princess?"

"Just forget you ever knew me."

"You sure you want me to do that?" He stared straight into my eyes, and without warning my stomach filled with wild butterflies.

"What is it now?" Taylor asked, hurrying down the stairs.

"Nothing," Thiago said, sitting back down beside Maggie.

"We could help out a little," she offered, looking at me with false sympathy. "I don't mind."

"We're fine, thanks," I responded.

I left the broom to help Taylor with the last couple of trash bags, and we went outside to leave them on the curb.

"I'll grab a quick shower and we can bounce, OK?" he said as we walked back up the stairs.

"Great," I said, falling back on his bed, where I should have wound up the night before. Where his lips should have kissed me passionately. Where his hands should have gripped me.

Why did I have to fuck everything up?

I took out my phone and looked at my Instagram again. Now that people could no longer comment on the photo with Kate that I'd deleted, they were insulting me through DMs. It was weird to me that Taylor hadn't brought it up. So I told him the whole story when he came out, a towel wrapped around his waist.

"Someone really hacked your account?" he asked.

"Yeah," I said as he sat down beside me. "Someone is trying

to mess with me, and I have no idea who it is. First the lockers, now this..."

"People are crazy. I'll tell you one thing, though. If I find out who's doing this, they won't try anything like it again. I swear."

"Don't worry about it, babe," I said, stroking his stubbly chin. "It's probably just some bored loser."

I didn't say anything about the weird account, @omv_ovamat, or the message from it. I don't know why. Maybe I didn't want to admit aloud how much people hated me. I was already ashamed enough, without having to add on all this extra bullshit. I saw Momo again in my mind, and I wished I could forget that creepy face and everything related to it.

Once Taylor had gotten dressed, we walked downstairs and drove straight to the library. I tried not to notice that Maggie's car was still there even though she and Thiago had disappeared together.

Of course, as luck would have it, half the student body was at the library that day. Midterms were coming up, and a lot of projects were due. It wasn't easy to get through my readings on female sexuality with Taylor right there next to me. He kept cracking jokes, but still, I found the information interesting. Did you know a large number of men still think the clitoris is an invention? Or that a lot more lesbians achieve orgasm than heterosexual women? Or that 68 percent of women have admitted to faking an orgasm at least once?

The more I read, the more fascinated I became, especially about the gaps in our understanding of female sexuality and sexuality in general. There were so many myths and so much prejudice about women's pleasure that I wanted to share all the statistics I'd discovered with everyone under the sun.

"Wait, so the clit is inside the body too?"

We were looking at a drawing describing how the clitoris

is an organ that measures four inches long and has more than 8,000 nerve endings. "I guess," I said in a low voice, looking at the drawing. "Look at this: It says, 'It wasn't until 1998 that Australia's first female urologist depicted the anatomy of the clitoris in its entirety. It is the only human organ designed exclusively for pleasure.'"

"And for reproduction, though, right?" Taylor said, reading along.

"No," I said. I had finished the paragraph before him. "That's the thing. For thousands of years, they've told women that the vagina only exists for reproduction. Nobody wanted to admit that the organ that gave us pleasure wasn't actually the vagina! Because, after all, women's sole purpose was to make babies, right?"

"Hey, don't get mad at me," he said, surprised by my tone.

"You can see why it bothers me though, right? That no one gave a shit about studying women's pleasure until 1998!"

"That's just the year one woman discovered one thing, it doesn't mean that…"

"You don't get it! Our pleasure was stolen! And you know why? Because men wanted us to think vaginal orgasms were the only kind so we'd believe we needed them to give us pleasure."

"C'mon, girls these days touch themselves more than we do."

"Yeah, good for us," I answered, still looking at the screen. "Look! The clitoris wasn't even included as a body part in high school textbooks until 2017!"

"Yeah, it's scandalous," Tay said.

I scowled at him. "This is serious!"

"It's interesting too. When people hear all this in class, they're going to flip out."

"That's my hope…"

I remembered my first time with Danny. What a dickhead. He

didn't bother touching me where he should have; he never asked if I liked it or if I'd had an orgasm. Nothing! Once he had come, the whole thing was over.

"Listen, I promise I'll give your clitoris all the attention it needs once you decide to let me get near it," he whispered, causing my cheeks to turn an intense red.

"It'll happen," I said, smiling.

"I guess that'll have to do," he said, shutting his laptop and yawning. "Man, I'm exhausted."

I was too. Studying the day after a party was the absolute worst. I put my things in my backpack and got ready to walk out, and just then, I saw Kate enter with Amanda and Lisa in tow. They all glared at me before walking off toward a table by the fireplace.

"They can't stand me," I said, wondering how things had gotten so out of hand.

"Forget them, babe," Taylor replied.

"I'm more worried about who's behind all this," I said, glaring at Danny, who'd been sitting at the next table over, ignoring us the entire time.

"You know who I saw him making out with yesterday, right?" Taylor asked.

"Yeah, Ellie."

"You got it." He slipped his laptop into its case and looked at me more seriously. "Does that bother you?"

"It bothers me that she hid it from me, but mostly I can't believe that she could feel attracted to him, knowing how he treated me."

"Maybe he's nice to her?"

I had been about to gather my books, but I stopped. "What? Are you saying it was my fault he's such an asshole to me?"

"Jesus, Kami, I didn't say anything like that. You're touchy as hell."

I sighed and closed my eyes a moment to get my head together. "Sorry, you're right. Do you want to go out for lunch?"

Slinging his backpack over his shoulder, Taylor pulled me close and kissed me on the lips. "Everything's going to be all right, Kami, I promise."

But it wouldn't. How could it be all right that my father had moved out of my house? That my parents were getting a divorce? That my friends didn't like me anymore? That some weirdo was stalking me and trying to make my life hell?

I knew Taylor had good intentions, but there was nothing he could do about all that.

We went for lunch at a burger joint, but we had to cut it short because I was working the afternoon shift. Taylor dropped me off at Mill's, and I was grateful that I could just work and ignore my problems. At least for a while. But just as I was about to count the cash drawer, in walked Danny with his friends.

"Sorry, we're closing," I said, noticing the stupid varsity jacket he always wore. Was it the only thing he owned?

"It says on the door you close at nine," he responded, looking at his friends and laughing.

"It's five to nine."

"Yeah, exactly." He clapped Harry on the back. Victor laughed, and they walked to the table farthest from the counter. Mrs. Mill walked out and looked at her wristwatch.

"Hey, kids," she called, a bashful smile on her face, "we're closing in five minutes."

"That means you're still open, right?" Danny replied nastily.

Mrs. Mill leaned on her cane. She'd been having back problems all week. I'd been doing virtually everything there because Mr. Mill was now bedbound. Didn't Danny realize how shitty it was to barge into a place five minutes before closing?

Mrs. Mill tried to smile, telling them, "I could make something quick if y'all like."

"What do you want, guys? I'll take the full breakfast with extra bacon and scrambled eggs."

"Same."

"Me too."

I hated him. But what could Mrs. Mill do? She had a business to run. So she took their order, and, as she passed, I told her not to worry: I'd make everything and lock up; she could go home.

The relief on her face made me hate those jerkoffs even more. "Are you sure, honey?" she asked.

I nodded with an uneasy smile. "Absolutely. Don't worry about it."

"Well, that's just wonderful, thank you. Don't forget to lock the back door too."

"I won't."

As Mrs. Mill left, I went into the kitchen to start cooking. I was so engrossed in the task that I jumped when I noticed Danny had found his way back to the kitchen.

"You can't be in here," I said. "Staff only."

"I just wanted to make sure you've got everything under control."

I stopped beating the eggs.

"You think I don't know how to make breakfast?"

Danny walked around the pastry table and leaned against it, crossing his arms and giving me one of those charming smiles I could no longer stand. "It's still hard to believe you had to get a job. What happened to the Kamila Hamilton everyone used to idolize? Do you have any idea how pathetic you look here?"

I ignored how much that hurt and fired back, "Do you have any idea how pathetic your mere existence is? Now get out." I pointed at the door.

"Your family is *actually* broke! The Hamilton dynasty in shambles!"

"Fuck off, moron," I said, on the verge of throwing the whisk at his head.

"You know, I'm kind of glad there's some psycho trying to ruin your life because if there weren't, I might do it myself. Watching you suffer is bringing me more pleasure than you could imagine." He smiled.

"Are you hearing yourself?"

"Loud and clear," he responded, and came closer. "You tried to fuck me over, and now it's your turn to go down... But, believe it or not, there's a part of me that's sad to see you go. I do still care about you. I mean, we did go out for two years, didn't we?"

"Yeah, I keep asking myself what I was high on back then." I had no idea what he was after. "What the fuck do you want, Danny?"

"I've got a proposition for you."

"I'm not interested," I said, turning back to my work.

But he kept talking as if he hadn't heard me: "Get back with me, and your life will be like it was before. You won't have to work in this dump or ride your bike to school anymore. No one will dare talk shit about you again. I'll even talk to my dad; maybe he can help out with your family's problems."

I didn't expect that. "What makes you think I'd even consider getting back with you?"

"Your life was way better while I was protecting you."

"Protecting me? Trust me, I don't need anyone to protect me."

"Oh, but you do. You think all the people talking shit about you now didn't feel this way last year or the year before? You were Little Miss Perfect, you had everything a high school kid could want, and there was a whole army of people who hated you for it, and now that things have gotten ugly for you, they can let their true colors show. With me around they were too scared, but not anymore."

I slammed the spatula on the counter. "I don't want a goddamn thing from you, Danny! I don't want your company, your money, your protection, your popularity! Nothing! Did you forget what you did to me?"

"That was just once!" Danny glowered.

"Twice, damn it! You hit me twice, you bastard!"

"Shut up!" he screamed, looking at the door, scared his friends would hear. "Just shut your fucking mouth."

"Why? Why would I? You keep talking about my reputation and how no one respects me and no one likes me, and why? Because my father got in trouble? Well, that's not my fault! You, though, the things you've done—"

"You ungrateful little bitch! I came here to—"

"You came here to blackmail me."

We both heard the doorbell chime and looked out toward the front. It was Julian. He peeked through the window into the kitchen and gave Danny a threatening look before asking me, "Is everything all right?"

"Yeah. Danny was just leaving."

"That's right," he said, looking at Julian with disgust. "I'll let your gay boyfriend have his time with you."

Danny walked out, and to my surprise, Julian didn't say anything to defend himself.

"I'm sorry," I said, approaching him.

"It's fine."

"It's not fine, he's an idiot. Don't pay attention to what he said."

"Well, I mean, I am gay, right? I don't care if people call me out for what I am."

"But…" I started, and he interrupted me.

"Seriously, Kam, don't worry. Are you OK?"

I heard the front door open again, and when I walked out to the counter, Danny, Harry, and Victor were leaving.

"I can't fucking believe this!" I looked at their half-cooked meals and started cursing.

"Aren't you supposed to be closed?" Julian asked. "It's nine twenty."

I sighed.

"Yeah, exactly. You feel like having breakfast for dinner?"

He shrugged as I put the last touches on the dishes and carried them out. At least tonight I wouldn't have to eat whatever slop my mother had come up with.

CHAPTER ELEVEN

Taylor

I DIDN'T WANT TO TELL KAMI THAT I KNEW ABOUT THE PHOTO OF her and Kate and all the comments people had left. That I'd seen what that weirdo @omv_ovamat had written.

NOW YOU'RE LIKE ME, AND SOON YOU'LL BE MINE.

What was that shit supposed to mean? How was she supposed to be like that fucking coward, whoever *they* were? I didn't know, but I wasn't going to sit back and watch while everybody made my girlfriend miserable. I knew if I asked Kami, she'd probably tell me to let her deal with it on her own, but that wasn't going to happen.

I called Perez, a friend of my brother's from back in DC. He was a computer freak, and I knew if anyone could find this asshole, he could. Perez wasn't a full-on hacker, but I was sure he could deal with a high school kid who thought they were being clever.

"Sure, dude," he said when I explained the situation. "I'll get right on it tomorrow. I've got another job to finish today, but I don't think it will take long."

"No worries," I said. Then I googled *Momo*. That mask was creepy as shit. I'd heard of the Momo Challenge. Supposedly there were videos on YouTube where Momo came on the screen to scare kids while they watched *Peppa Pig* or whatever and forced them to do things against their will, threatening to hurt their families or something if they didn't. It had gone viral, then it turned out to be an urban legend, and I kind of lost track of the story after that. What was the connection between that image, whoever @omv_ovamat was, and my girlfriend?

"TAYLOR!"

Shit.

I closed my laptop as Mom charged into my room like a bat out of hell.

"Have you seen this damn house?" she shouted, throwing the door open so hard it struck the wall.

"I cleaned up…"

"There are condoms in my room! Used condoms!"

"What are you talking about?"

My mom was small and elegant. My brother and I were well over a foot taller than her, and yet, when she wanted to, she could scare the hell out of us.

"You get in there and clean it right now! And you better wash my sheets too!" She slapped me on the back of the neck.

"Jesus!" I shouted. "I told everyone the bedrooms were off limits."

"I give you an inch, and you take a mile. You told me you were going to have a few friends over…"

"That's all I did!"

She gave me a dirty look.

"I'll clean it up, all right?"

"Damn right you will! Now get to it!"

I walked out and started cleaning…again. One thing was for certain: I'd never have another party again. I hadn't even had a good time. Not after learning about my brother's childhood infatuation with Kami, not after our fight, and definitely not after

Julian stuck his nose in it. That motherfucker got on my nerves. What was his deal? He was supposedly gay, but the way he hung all over Kami made me wonder, were they really just friends? I didn't get what the hell was going on.

It had been four hours since I'd dropped Kami off at Mill's. She was supposed to call me when her shift was over, and we were going to grab dinner and maybe watch a movie. Nothing too late because we had class the next day. I checked my phone, and it was like someone had been reading my mind: Hey, I can't do dinner. Trouble at work. I'll tell you later. Julian's taking me home.

What was Julian doing at the café?

Honestly, ever since I'd started going out with Kami, it had been one problem after another. My brother and I barely talked. And I wasn't sure why, but it was definitely connected to Kami. Did Thiago like her? I knew he had when we were kids, but that was ages ago. And now he had Maggie, the cute teacher.

So why did there seem to be some sort of vibe between Thiago and Kami, then? Was I just imagining things?

I went to bed early. I had a hangover, and all that cleaning and studying had worn me out. I slept like a baby. The next morning, when I got up, my room was freezing. It was only early November, but my teeth were chattering. I looked outside and saw it was pouring rain. Fucking Monday.

It was still dark outside, and I hated getting up that early, but I got dressed anyway. When I went downstairs, Mom was still asleep, but my brother was making coffee in the kitchen. He was wearing a sweater and boots, like me.

"You see how cold it is?" I asked him.

"According to my phone, it's right at freezing," he said, pouring us each a cup. "You want some scrambled eggs?"

"Sure, I'll make them, though," I said, grabbing four eggs out of the fridge.

"You think it'll snow?" Thiago asked, peering out the window.

"I hope not," I said, starting to beat the eggs.

"What the..." Thiago said. He sounded both incredulous and indignant at the same time. I looked outside. Kami had just walked out her door. She was in a wool cap and a puffer coat, and I was pretty sure she was wheeling out her bike.

"Is she trying to freeze to death? Why is she so dumb sometimes?" my brother asked no one in particular.

"You finish this up," I said, "I'll go get her." I put down the fork and bowl of eggs and went outside. The wind hit me right in the face, cold and painful.

"Hey!" I shouted, and she turned around just before hopping on her bike. "You are kidding me, right?" I walked over to her with big strides.

"Hey there," she said with that smile that had made me fall in love with her. God, how I loved her. "It sure is cold, isn't it?"

"Yeah, it's fucking cold. I can see that, but I'm not sure you can. Where are you planning to go on that bicycle?"

"To school, where else? I decided to leave early because it'll take me a bit longer with the wind in my face."

"Kami, I'll take you," I said.

"No! Seriously." She shook her head. "You don't have to drive me around all the time. I'm in the mood for a ride, anyway, I need some fresh air—"

"Frozen air, you mean. Put down that heap of junk and come inside for a cup of coffee."

Kam looked at the house and shook her head.

"No, seriously, I'm fine."

"Kamila, either you come of your own accord or I'm dragging you. I'm not going to let you get pneumonia when I have a car with heat and I can drive you. Come on."

She really seemed resistant, and I asked again if she honestly wanted to ride a bike through that storm.

"Fine," she said, leaning her bike against the wall. "But don't think this is going to be an everyday thing. I can ride my bike fine, I just need to bundle up and—"

"Whatever." I grabbed her hand and pulled her with me. "Jesus, it's freezing," I said.

Kami stood in the entrance shivering as I closed the door. "What the hell's up with you?" I asked. "Get in the kitchen where it's warm and drink some coffee already."

She sighed as she came in. Thiago had already made the eggs and was taking out a mug for her. "You trying to get hypothermia?" he asked.

"Could you two stop blowing everything out of proportion, please!"

"Whatever. Here, drink this," Thiago told her, passing her a steaming cup. Kami grabbed it, and the three of us sat down at the table.

"Maybe we should just stay home," I said, breaking the silence. Why were they both being so weird around each other? Was I really going to have to deal with this again?

"It does look like it might snow," Thiago said.

"I checked the weather," I replied, "but it didn't say anything."

"If it snows, you guys know what that means, right?" Kami said.

Thiago and I looked at her—neither of us did.

"Don't tell me you guys forgot?"

"There is no fucking way they're still..." I started to say.

"The bonfires!" she shouted. "Of course we still have them! First snowfall of the year always means bonfires, marshmallows, cookies, hot chocolate, good music, and—"

"Booze," I interrupted her. "Yeah, I remember."

Kami rolled her eyes. "It's not just about drinking, it's about having fun. It's honestly one of my favorite Carsville festivities."

"Do they still have a competition for best snowman?"

"Yeah, but now only kids can take part."

"What the hell?" I asked.

"But if we get my little brother to sign up, we can help," Kami said, with excitement in her eyes. I'd forgotten how much she liked the snow, sledding, snowmen, bonfires... We'd had some good winter times together when we were little, and I was happy to be able to relive that with her.

"Let it snow!"

The three of us left our mugs in the sink and got in the car to head to school. As soon as we walked in, we saw a giant poster welcoming us in the hallway right by the lockers.

University Week, it said.

"Is it really this week?" Kami asked.

"Is what this week?" I responded.

"Have fun, kids," my brother smirked, walking off toward the teachers' lounge with one quick look back at Kami. I don't know if I was imagining things, if I was paranoid or what, but I was sure I kept seeing something between them. I didn't like it, and it was starting to affect my mood.

"Taylor, how do you not know about this? We have our practice SATs, there are special classes about how to write an application essay, recruiters from different colleges come to visit. Shit..." She stopped at a long table covered in flyers and read the words *Ivy League*. Behind it were the flags of the eight best colleges in the country: Brown, Columbia, Cornell, Dartmouth, Harvard, UPenn, Princeton, and Yale.

"Fuckfuckfuck," she said, picking up a leaflet with a blue cover and the logo for Yale.

I couldn't help but smile at how worked up she got. "Sometimes I forget how soon it is until we go off to college."

"There's no way I'm getting in," she said, squeezing the brochure so tight it started to crumple. "There's just no way..."

"Don't be an idiot," I said, taking it from her hands. "You're one of the top students."

"Right. *One of*. But not *the best*."

"I think you're the best," I said, trying to encourage her.

"I'm not getting in. I already know it." There was panic in her beautiful brown eyes.

"Hey! Calm down. You've got plenty of time still, don't start obsessing now."

She picked the flyer up and started reading it again. My eyes drifted over to the materials for Harvard. I reached for the flyer, but someone else's hand picked it up first. It was Ellie, Kami's best friend.

"So you're the competition?" I asked her.

She narrowed her eyes. I don't know why, but I felt like she was always giving me nasty looks. "For me, there is no competition. I'm getting in, and that's that," she replied.

"Is that so? I guess that's why you're hanging out with that douchebag, to improve your chances? Because unless his parents pull strings for you, I don't really see it happening."

"Shut up, dumbass."

"Oh, that really is it!" Now I saw I'd touched a nerve. It was known that Danny's family had lots of money and lots of connections, and they were generous with the people they liked. "I wondered what would drive you to hook up with your best friend's ex even after you learned he was an abuser."

"There's a lot you don't know, Taylor."

"Like what?"

"Ellie!" Kami said, walking toward us. "Did you see all the new brochures?" She was gushing, but then she stopped, and her tone changed when she saw how tense we were. "Is something up?"

"Nope," Ellie responded. "Just your boyfriend sticking his nose in where it doesn't belong." She glared at me. What the hell had I done to her, anyway?

"I'm just trying to clear up a few things I don't quite understand," I said.

"Curiosity killed the cat, my friend," Ellie quipped.

"Touché," I said, surprised by her sarcasm.

Just then, the bell rang. Ellie told Kami she'd see her in history class and hurried off. Then a voice came from behind me.

"Are you going to class?" Julian again. Didn't he realize he and I weren't friends? Not after his talking shit about Thiago and Kami at my party. And especially not after him stopping in at my girlfriend's work and picking her up on a night we were supposed to hang out. I wanted to tell him straight up that I couldn't stand him, but I held back, for Kami's sake. She seemed genuinely glad to see him.

The first three hours of class were eternal, and I was glad when it was time for gym. I dressed and was surprised to see my brother sitting on the bleachers when I walked out of the locker room. That was weird—he usually taught the younger kids, while Coach Klebb ran our classes.

"Listen up, everyone," he said when we were all gathered. "Some of you may have heard this, but Coach Klebb is retiring." None of us had heard, and everyone started murmuring. I looked around for Kami and found her on the opposite end of the room, her eyes focused on Thiago.

Coach Klebb was gone?

"I know, I know. It's a shock, everybody liked him, but the school has offered me his post. It's temporary—they're looking for a permanent candidate—but that doesn't mean I won't be taking this job seriously. I'll be working you harder than ever."

Again, people glanced around and whispered to each other. Personally, I was happy that my brother had been picked for the job. I knew he would do us good.

"As you all know," he said, "I'm a basketball guy, so that's what we're going to play today. We're going to break up into six small teams, and we'll have ten-minute turns, with the winner staying in."

In my mind, I was already tallying up my best players: Harry, Julian, Marty, maybe...

"We're doing mixed teams, and I'll pick the players," Thiago announced. There went all my plans.

"Fuck that!" Danny shouted. For the first time in my life, I agreed with him. "I don't want a bunch of girls on my team."

With an icy stare, my brother said, "Cool, you won't have to worry about it. You can stay on the sidelines doing burpees and jumping jacks."

I couldn't help but grin.

This was going to be fun.

CHAPTER TWELVE

Kami

THE GIRLS' BASKETBALL SKILLS WERE INVERSELY PROPORTIONAL TO their cheerleading ability. Me included. Our school had a reputation for putting out good basketball players, and the guys pretty much all knew what they were doing, but we girls weren't only flubbing it, we were getting in the way.

"Move," someone named Richie shouted at me—I don't think I'd ever seen him in my life—and he elbowed past me before setting up his jump shot.

Taylor was on his team, but he still defended me. "That was a foul!"

"Taylor," Thiago shouted, "are you honestly going to snitch on your own teammates?" I could tell he was relishing his new position of authority.

"Didn't you see how he nearly knocked her over?"

He was so protective of me, I was touched, and I ran over to kiss him on the cheek and tell him I was fine. Thiago yelled, "Hamilton, this is a game, not date night."

I stepped away from my boyfriend and got back into position. Soon enough, our team lost, and we had to go sit on the bench.

Taylor's team had yet to lose a game, and we all took turns trying to beat them. Meanwhile, Danny, on the sidelines, looked like he was about to explode. He kept yelling, "Not that way, dumbass! Over there!" and harassing this poor girl from our art class. She was a skinny, short thing with thick glasses, and she froze every time someone passed her the ball.

"Walker! Drop and give me twenty!" Thiago demanded every time Danny opened his mouth. That was his line—he'd even made me do some, first for jumping on Taylor's back when he was supposed to be blocking me but instead reached back and tickled me, and second for flipping the bird at Julian, who kept dribbling around me in a circle to piss me off because he knew there was nothing I could do to stop him.

I couldn't help but laugh as I saw Danny sweating and grunting. He deserved it—he deserved that and worse. During a water break, I walked over to Taylor and smiled.

"Are you sure you want to be an engineer?" I asked him. He grabbed me around the waist and picked me up. "Because you look sexy as hell out there on the court," I added.

"Give me a kiss right now, and I'll be whatever you want me to be," he said, and leaned in. I couldn't help but open my eyes as Taylor put his tongue in my mouth, and I was not surprised to see Thiago watching us. And he didn't seem too happy about it.

"Back on the court!" he shouted, without taking his eyes off me.

Taylor let me go with one last peck on the cheek, and jogged out on the court. I sat next to Ellie on the bleachers. She still hadn't told me what was going on with her and Danny.

"Hey," I said, trying to figure out how I could confront the issue without sounding jealous. "What happened with you and Danny at the Halloween party?"

Blushing slightly, she said curtly, "Why do you ask?"

Should I tell her I saw her, I wondered, or just keep asking questions to see if she'd admit it herself?

"I mean, I saw you guys," I said, deciding to cut to the point.

"Saw us…?" She was playing dumb.

"I saw you kissing him, Ellie."

She looked over at Danny, who was back in the game, dribbling the ball down the court. "Can't we just pretend it didn't happen?" she asked, turning back to me. Her cheeks were flushed from the cold, and her black lashes made the dark circles under her eyes look more dramatic.

"But why did you do it? Do you like him?"

She hesitated. "You know, Kami, you can't always control who you fall in love with."

"You're in love with him?!" I shouted, unable to help myself.

"Hamilton, that's ten more push-ups," Thiago called from the sidelines, turning to face me.

Goddammit! "I didn't do anything!" I stood and shouted.

"You're supposed to be paying attention, not gossiping."

"What am I supposed to pay attention to?"

"The game. Just because your team isn't playing right now doesn't mean you can goof off," he said, completely ignoring the fact that everyone else was talking too.

"I can talk and pay attention at the same time!" I wasn't in the mood for more push-ups.

"Sorry," Thiago responded. "Let's make that twenty."

I stomped over to him. "You're pushing it way too far, Thiago," I whispered, so only he could hear me.

"You can call me *Coach* or *Mr. Di Bianco*, not *Thiago*." He turned back to the court. "Walker, pass the ball!"

"You've been testing me ever since class started," I said. I was annoyed by his attitude and refused to do any more push-ups.

"You've been getting on my nerves today more than normal," he said. "Now give me those push-ups, and not the half-assed, knees-on-the-ground kind—count 'em out."

"I hate you," I said.

"Good. That solves a serious problem then," he said, looking me straight in the eye.

"What problem?"

"Me pulling you off into an empty classroom and fucking you against the chalkboard, for example."

My mouth went suddenly dry. I couldn't believe he'd just said that. "What?"

"I said, twenty push-ups!" he screamed. I noticed Taylor was watching us out of the corner of his eye. I walked off in a state of shock and found a place to do my push-ups. It wasn't until Ellie told me I was on number twenty-five that I realized I was in a completely different world. How could he say that to me? In the middle of class? Just like that?

After class, I hurried first into the locker room, changed quickly, and then sat outside watching the other girls come and go. Ellie came out soon after and asked me to go with her to lunch, but I said I had a headache and might go to the nurse's office for some aspirin. I told her if she saw Taylor, to tell him I'd be there in a few minutes. I knew Thiago would still be in the gym, putting away the equipment. The coach was always the last to leave, and he had to check to make sure no one had left anything behind. I kept sitting there, and eventually he made his rounds and returned. He didn't seem remotely surprised to find me there.

"What are you doing here?" he asked.

"Waiting for you." My heart beat faster. There was nothing I could do to force it to behave in the presence of my boyfriend's brother.

"You're not supposed to be here unsupervised. I could give you detention for this."

That's when my mind spun out of control. To a place where a phrase like that was more of a turn-on than a threat. Thiago seemed to read my thoughts, and his voice dropped from a deep, imposing baritone to a whisper as he told me, "Kamila, you need to leave."

"You can't treat me that way in front of everyone," I said. I needed him to know that he had hurt me.

"I can treat you however I want. I'm the teacher and you're the student, remember?"

"Do you tell other students you want to fuck them?"

"Go to class."

"No." I crossed my arms.

"Kamila..."

"Aren't we going to talk about what happened at your house two days ago?" I said.

"Nope," he replied, leaning against a wall and crossing his own arms.

I was furious. "What we did meant nothing to you, did it?" I asked.

"You seemed to like it," he replied.

"Don't act like I'm the only one who wanted it," I said.

"What if you were?"

"Oh, right, after all you've got your teacher friend, Miss what's-her-name..." I said sarcastically.

"Maggie."

"Oh, whatever, I don't give a shit about her name." I fell silent for a moment. "I hate this."

"You hate what?"

"This," I said, pointing back and forth between us. "Me being with your brother. I shouldn't feel like this. I shouldn't..."

"You shouldn't what?"

"I shouldn't want to be with both of you!"

It wasn't until I said it aloud that I realized it was true. Yes: I had feelings for both of them. It wasn't just a passing infatuation. It wasn't just a slip-up, or that I was attracted to Thiago. I had feelings for him. And I had feelings for Taylor too.

Thiago's face was perfectly still. I had no idea what was going on inside him. Was it possible that I was just a plaything for him? Someone to give him a blow job at a fucking costume party?

"I hate seeing you with him," he finally confessed.

Once more, I froze, taking a deep breath and trying to calm the storm inside me caused by those simple words. "Well, I don't like seeing you with Maggie."

"That's a problem, isn't it?" He moved closer. He was only a few steps away now. "Thiago..."

"Do you have any idea what it feels like when I hear you say my name?"

"It shouldn't make you feel anything! Isn't that what you've been trying to tell me, that you feel nothing?" I made sure I was looking him dead in the eye when I said it.

"I'm no good for you, Kamila," he said, patting my cheek. "And you don't deserve my brother."

Those words broke something inside me. Because he was right. Maybe not about whether he was good for me, but as for whether I deserved Taylor...of course I didn't. "I have feelings for him, though...I really do," I said. I didn't know what exactly those feelings were, but there was something about Taylor that...

"To hell with your feelings. You cheated on him. With me. More than once," he said. "As much as I hate to admit it, I know there's a part of you that loves him and wants to make him happy, but this isn't how you go about it, Kamila. What happened the other night..."

"Shouldn't have happened," I said, trying to get my thoughts in order.

"But it did happen...and in a way, I think I was trying to push you to see how far you'd go with me. And if my brother hadn't burst in on us, I know we'd have gone all the way."

Almost reflexively, I pushed him away.

"You *pushed* me to see how far I'd go?"

"Did I stutter?"

"You were pretending with me?"

"Kam, you can't play both of us. You should just stay away. I'm your teacher. God knows what would happen if anything about us came out. And my brother... He deserves someone who won't go around giving other guys blow jobs behind his back. Especially his own brother."

Those words stung. They hurt like daggers plunging into my heart. And I was furious, and the fury blazed, but it also gave me strength, the strength to tell that asshole he'd better watch who he was talking to. I pushed him again, and he grabbed my wrists.

"You didn't seem to care much about your brother the other night. You were begging for it!"

"Because I'm a piece of shit! I told you I don't deserve you, and that's why! Nobody should love me! Not even my brother!"

"I guess that's supposed to be some kind of justification?"

"Kami, you can do better, I know it," he said, still holding me tightly. "Prove to me that I didn't fall in love with the wrong person."

He didn't let me say anything else. He didn't let me push him or punch him or kiss him. Nothing. He let me go, turned around, and walked off.

———

Guilt plagued me as I walked into the cafeteria and saw Taylor. How could I? How could I have just cheated on him like it was nothing? What was wrong with me? Thiago was right: I was a bad person. I wished he had put it in different words, but he was right. I didn't deserve to be with Taylor. It was natural for him to look out for his brother. I needed to become someone better. I needed to change. And I would. But could I do it without Taylor?

"Hey, blondie," he said as I walked over to his table. "I went ahead and got you a tray. I was worried they'd shut down the line before you got here."

There I was, fantasizing about his brother while he was worried about whether I would get anything to eat.

"Thanks," I said, sitting down next to him. I couldn't help but notice all of our friends, even Ellie, were sitting elsewhere.

"I wanted to be alone with you," he said, pulling me in for a quick kiss.

Tensely, I told him, "Listen, I don't want you cutting yourself off from the group for my sake. I don't mind eating alone, honestly."

"I'd never let you eat alone," he said, shocked by the idea.

He didn't deny that it was my fault they didn't want to sit with him. I was an outcast now, and his being with me made him an outcast too. Taylor didn't deserve that, dammit. He deserved to be the center of attention, the life of the party, the king of the dance floor.

"What's up with you?" he asked me. He could tell I was being distant. Of course I was. I was a million miles away. "Ellie said something was wrong…"

"I'm fine."

"Hey!" I heard Julian coming up behind us. When I turned to see him, I noticed a huge smile on his face as he pointed outside. "Snow!" He said it so loudly, everyone in the cafeteria turned their heads.

And it was true. Outside we could see the first snowflakes of the year swirling slowly to the ground, beautiful against the gray sky. Taylor smiled just as some kid I didn't know climbed up on a table and shouted, "No school tomorrow," and the whole cafeteria broke into whistles and applause.

Everyone was celebrating. The Bonfire Fest was one of the oldest traditions in town and was always held the day after the first snow, even if it meant canceling classes. The cafeteria turned to chaos. People mulled around from table to table, chatting, laughing, and planning what they would do the next day. The happiness was so contagious, even I felt a little bit better.

"So...see you at the Bonfire Fest?" Julian asked, brimming with excitement as he sat down across from us.

"For sure," I said. But then I remembered something. "Shit! I have to help Mrs. Mill bake cakes and cookies. I forgot she asked me to lend a hand for the festival."

That was part of the tradition: local businesses donated food, sweets, and drinks, and everything was free for all the townspeople.

"So you're not going to be there?" Taylor asked, disappointed.

"I'm sure Mrs. Mill is planning to have everything ready by morning. I'll be there, I promise."

"Cool!"

"So we'll all hang out tomorrow?" Julian asked, looking at me enthusiastically.

"Sure..." I replied.

Taylor announced that he'd bring the booze. "It's supposed to be a party, isn't it?"

Julian frowned in response. He asked if I'd be drinking too, and I said that if someone got me a cup of mulled wine from Leo's, I wouldn't refuse it.

"That's my girl." Taylor kissed me on the cheek and stood up. He wanted to talk to his friends. "You gonna stay here with this dude?" he asked, referring to Julian.

Julian was still scowling, but he didn't seem to register Taylor's nasty tone in reference to him.

"Yeah, I'll stay here with *my friend*," I said. After Taylor had left, I took a bite of my sandwich and turned back to Julian. I started talking about how much fun the bonfire would be. Anything to avoid thinking about what had happened with Thiago a few minutes before.

"Listen, Kam," Julian murmured, leaning across the table so only I could hear him. "I don't know if I should tell you this, but..." He looked around to both sides.

"What?" I asked, curious and a little cautious.

"I heard you earlier." He was looking me straight in the eye.

I tensed. "You heard what?" I was trying to buy time to make excuses, to come up with something that might justify my argument with Thiago and how I had cheated on his brother... with him.

"I heard you with Thiago, honey." He shrugged. "Not like it takes a genius to figure out something's been going on between you two. I had left something in my locker and was going back for it, but then I stopped at the door when I heard you. You're lucky it was me; anyone else and y'all would be screwed."

Suddenly it dawned on me that if what we'd done got out, Taylor wouldn't be the only one upset about it. If the principal heard, Thiago would lose his job, and then what would he do?

"Julian..." I could feel the palms of my hands starting to sweat.

"Relax," he said with a gentle smile. "I told you, I saw this coming, but you need to be careful, Kamila." He'd never called me by my full name before, and it sounded strange coming from his mouth, distant. "People hate you now, and they're not going to like it when they find out you're hooking up with both brothers— the two hottest guys at the school. Trust me, it won't make you popular; they'll use it to tear you down."

People hate you now...

I looked around.

How had I ended up so alone?

I stood, and Julian took my hand.

"Babe," he said, stroking my palm, "I'm telling you all this for your own good. I'm not judging you. Fuck, I understand. Who wouldn't struggle to choose between those two? But you need to watch out..."

"I know," I said, trying not to cry. "And thanks. I'm gonna go. I've got to finish my math homework." I didn't wait for an answer. I just turned around and walked out, feeling the stares of the other students on my back like a firing squad taking aim at me.

I didn't want Taylor and Thiago to give me a ride home. As soon as the bell rang, I grabbed my books and ran out. It was a long walk, but I didn't care. I didn't even care that it was cold and snowing.

I sent Taylor a message telling him I'd gotten a ride with Julian and that I'd see him the next day, and I took a path into the woods. There was snow everywhere, on the ground, weighing down the branches of the trees, and I was able to admire the beauty of it despite the chaos in my life. The solitude helped me think. To reflect. To try to figure out what I wanted and what I needed.

It was obvious my feelings for both guys were real. But was it normal to fall in love with two guys at once? Was I in love with Thiago? What I felt for him was more physical, a hopeless attraction that made me want to lose control, whereas Taylor... Taylor made me feel all kinds of things. Safe, protected, loved, valued, attractive...Taylor made me feel special, dammit.

What had happened with Thiago was the accumulation of suppressed rage and an intense physical attraction, but all that could fizzle out.

Whereas Taylor... I didn't want things to end with him. I didn't want to give him up.

Who was Thiago to make me feel the way he had in the gym? He was worse than I was. But love and attraction didn't follow any rules.

Everything we'd always been taught was *correct* had changed now. Traditionally, it was only acceptable for one man and one woman to fall in love. And now look how much things had changed...Women could fall in love with other women, men with other men... Now there was polyamory, throuples, bisexuality. Was it so bad, then, to have feelings for two guys?

I knew I wasn't a bad person. I'd made my mistakes, but at the same time, how can what you feel be mistaken? Feelings aren't rational; they know no laws. Feelings are feelings; they exist and that's that. And there's nothing you can do to make them magically vanish. Control them, maybe; hide them, sure; but judge them? I wasn't going to let anyone make me feel bad because I had feelings for two amazing guys. But I wasn't going to be self-serving and try to justify what I'd done either. I had a right to my feelings, and nobody could criticize me for them, but what I'd done with Thiago had been wrong. Really, what I was doing with both of them was wrong because I was betraying them both: one to his face and the other behind his back.

I hadn't arrived at any real conclusions by the time I got home, I was just more confused and colder than ever. But that wasn't the worst thing. Nope, it was the car I saw parked in the driveway.

Please, no.

Even as I stuck the key in the lock, I was hesitant. I could always turn back. I could go sleep in the tree house. I probably wouldn't freeze to death, right?

"Kamila!" That voice. It was like nails on a chalkboard, and I heard it even before the door opened. "You honestly thought it was a good idea to walk all the way across town in this weather?"

My grandmother. My mother's mother. There she was before me, with her bleached-blond hair pulled back in an elegant bun, her face stretched tight after who knew how many facelifts, her black pants and her cashmere sweater with those pearls she probably didn't even take off to get in the shower...

"Grandma," I said, wanting to run away. "What are you doing here?"

"What do you mean, what am I doing here? Helping your mother, obviously. Now get in here before you catch cold."

I shut the door behind me, asking, "Where's Grandpa?" as I looked around.

"Your grandfather couldn't come this time. It's just me," she responded with a frown. "Kamila, your mother's a wreck. I thought you'd be old enough to start to shoulder some of the burden, but according to her, all you think about is yourself, and you're acting like a spoiled brat. Did you forget you're an eighteen-year-old woman now?"

"Grandma..." I said, taking off my jacket, but she interrupted me.

"Don't you dare *Grandma* me. I came here to help you crawl out of the black hole your father got you all into, and we're going to get started right away. To begin with, you will quit your job at that dinky little café."

I paused on my way up to my room. "I won't, but thanks for the suggestion," I said, unable to believe I was stuck there arguing with a version of my mom from the 1980s.

"You will, or else your grandfather and I won't be paying for your college. You're planning on going to Yale—you should be studying, not working!"

"I don't want your money!"

"How do you plan on paying for school then?"

"There are scholarships. In fact, I've already planned on applying for one."

My mother appeared through the kitchen door. "There's no point in trying, Mom, it's like talking to a brick wall."

"Yeah, well, this brick wall needs to get some shut-eye," I said. I cared so little at this point, I wasn't even offended.

"It's almost dinnertime!" my grandmother said, crossing her arms. "And this conversation is not over, little lady!"

I didn't answer. I just went to my room, shut the door, and locked it. Then I sat down at my desk, took out my sketch pad, and started to draw. Art had always been my therapy. No matter what happened, it was there for me. Canvas, paper—even a napkin would do—and a pen, a pencil, or paint.

After an hour, I had drawn an image of a girl, tears streaming down a face uncannily similar to my own. I looked up, and there was Thiago looking at me from his window. It was almost as if he had tapped me on the shoulder to get my attention. I held his gaze for a moment. Then I decided this was enough. Thiago had toyed with me. He had tested me. He had taken advantage of my feelings, and then he'd tried to make me feel guilty for it. I couldn't believe he'd dared to tell me to leave his brother alone because *I* wasn't good enough for him. I was exhausted from thinking about it. I raised my hand, flipped him off, and pulled my curtains shut.

Thiago Di Bianco wasn't going to tell me what I could and couldn't do.

He was probably the last person in the world who had the right to do so.

CHAPTER THIRTEEN

Kami

A TEXT MESSAGE COMING THROUGH WOKE ME UP. I OPENED ONE eye and felt around for my iPhone. But since I couldn't find it, I sat up and turned on the light.

"Fuck!" I threw aside the covers, looked under the pillows. "Where are you?"

When I looked under the bed, I saw it had fallen through the crack between the bed and the wall while I was asleep, meaning I'd have to get on my hands and knees and reach under the bed as far as I could through the accumulated dust to grab it.

Once I was up again, I started coughing. Now that Prue no longer came to clean, the house had become a disaster. Between work and school, I barely had time for anything else, and domestic duties were the last thing my mother cared about. Did she think dirt and grime just magically disappeared? I grunted and sat on the bed. The message was from Mrs. Mill.

Honey, I need you here at eight. We've got to prepare for the Bonfire Fest. I'll pay you overtime.

No surprises there.

Before tossing my phone on the bed and hopping into the shower, I had to open my Instagram one more time. I wished I could resist, but it's just a fact of life for anyone born after 2000. Ever since my account was hacked, I had changed all my passwords: email, Facebook, Instagram, TikTok…

In my friends' stories, I was surprised to find out there had been a party at Kate's house the night before. Her parents were usually insanely strict, but what hurt the most was how everyone I knew, almost our entire class, had been at that spontaneous party. And I hadn't heard a word about it.

I saw Ellie in the crowd, dancing and drinking. Of course it broke my heart. Still worse, Julian had to have known about it because he lived there too. But he'd kept the whole thing from me. As I flicked through the images, there was a knock at my door.

"Kami, can I come in?" my brother asked.

When I opened the door, he was standing there very still, clutching his iguana. His eyes were teary, and he threw himself into my arms.

"Kami, I don't want her to die," he said, squeezing the poor lizard so tightly, I was worried he'd kill it himself.

"Cam, Juana's not going to die," I said, pulling him inside and shutting the door.

"But she is…" he said, wiping away his tears and trembling.

"Buddy, I promise you Juana's going to be fine. Take a deep breath, OK? Come here." I picked him up and set him down on the bed, then put the giant lizard next to us, trying to keep my mind off the fact that Juana was splayed out across the very sheets where I slept. My brother now broke into sobs. "What makes you think she's going to die?" I asked.

"She said she was going to kill him," he whispered, almost as if he were afraid someone would hear him. A shiver ran down my spine.

"Who, Cam? Who said that?" I grabbed him and shook him.

He looked around—I couldn't imagine why he was so paranoid. "She'll hurt me if I tell you." He was trying as hard as he could to be brave, but he just couldn't handle it. I could see pure panic in his eyes.

I grabbed his face and held it and looked him straight in the eye as calmly as I could. "Listen to me, OK? No one, and I mean no one, is ever going to hurt you. Not you, and not your iguana."

"But she said..."

"She? Who is she?" I asked, thinking maybe at last I'd learn who was bullying my brother.

Cameron leaned in toward my ear and whispered so softly I could barely hear him, making clear to me at last that what had been happening to me at school was related to everything my little brother had been going through.

"Momo," he said, hugging me as if even uttering that name aloud made him want to run away and hide.

I shivered and visualized that terrifying face, but I kept my cool. This was ridiculous, after all.

"Cameron, Momo isn't real."

"She is real, Kami. She exists. She said that Mom and Dad would get divorced if I didn't do what she said. But I don't want to do what she says. I don't want to hurt anyone!"

Jesus. "Cameron, what did she ask you to do?"

He shook his head and started crying again. "I can't tell you."

"Cam, at school, Thiago and your teacher told me George Walker was bothering you..."

He nodded. "Yeah, but it's not his fault. Momo's making him do it."

"Did he tell you that?"

"He told me Momo would come for all of us if we didn't do what she said. And Momo doesn't like you. Momo wants bad things to happen to you. Momo's the one who told me to take your phone… And Momo made me give away your photos…"

"What?" I stood. "What photos, Cameron?" As I interrogated him, I walked over to my desk, looking for the box where I kept all my old photos—photos of myself with friends, private photos. And it wasn't there. "Who did you give the box to?"

I could tell my brother felt terrible about what he'd done, but he was so scared. "George," he said.

Unbelievable. So the little brother of my ex-boyfriend was behind this: the same ex-boyfriend who had sworn to ruin my life if I wouldn't get back together with him. "Cameron, this Momo bullshit is over as of tonight. I promise you that. No one is going to threaten you or scare you again. All right?"

He didn't seem very convinced.

How the hell could Danny stoop so low that he'd bring a six-year-old kid into this? He knew where the box of photos was, of course. There were lots of photos of us in there. He must have been having a ball watching me suffer, the jerk. Fucking with me, that was one thing. But my little brother? He had no idea who he was messing with.

I spent the morning in the café baking cakes and brownies, making sandwiches, blending batter for the muffins. By two in the afternoon, I was exhausted.

Mrs. Mill told me to take a break for half an hour, and she gave me a tuna sandwich and pointed to the door. I didn't need her to say it twice. I threw on my coat, grabbed my sandwich, and walked outside, ready to soak up the good cheer of the Bonfire Fest. Posters and lights had been strung up all over. The entire town did its part; everyone wanted the night to be magical. It was supposed to snow until midafternoon, leaving the night calm but chilly, with a beautiful blanket of white snow atop it. For the first snow to hit so early, in November, was unusual, but you never knew what to expect anymore in this crazy world.

I walked through Carsville and remembered years past: gathering beside a bonfire, even building one; toasting marshmallows; making s'mores... Kate loved the Bonfire Fest. She used to say that the sight of fire took her back in time and she could just stare into the flames for hours. I got that; bonfires had a similar effect on me. I don't know what it was, but gathering around the fire with your best friends was just special somehow.

I remember with Danny we used to stay until everyone else had left. He was sweet and attentive back then; he'd let me lie back with my head in his lap and comb his fingers through my hair until I'd nearly fallen asleep. Once, I remember him picking me up and carrying me to his car to drive me home. He had to shake me awake and tell me to go to my room before my parents had a heart attack.

Danny had always struggled to keep a grip on himself. That wasn't news to anybody, but treating me this way? It was weird. He was always impulsive, rash, but he had never been the type to deliberately manipulate a little kid so people would hate me.

I walked around as I ate the sandwich Mrs. Mill had given me. Thankfully, she'd let me off the hook that evening—she and her husband would watch the stall, the way they always had, and I could have fun.

I crossed the square to buy a Coke from the corner store. Julian was coming out with Kate, but they were arguing heatedly and didn't notice me.

"It's over, Julian," she said.

"Kate, you can't do this to me," he whined.

Kate frowned, seemingly disgusted by what he was saying. Then she saw me. Her face and Julian's both changed. Julian smiled softly and said, "Hey, Kam. Out for a walk?"

Did he honestly think I hadn't seen those videos of him and everyone else having the time of their lives at a party I hadn't been invited to? I realized the rest of them had written me off by that point, but Julian was supposed to be my friend.

"I'm just on break from the café," I said, noticing Kate was doing everything she could not to look at me.

"I'm outta here," she announced, jerking away from Julian, who hadn't seemed to notice that he was still gripping her arm.

The look he shot her made it clear that the conversation they'd been having wasn't over, but he turned back and devoted all his attention to me. "We fight a lot. I guess it's normal between brothers and sisters."

I couldn't stop staring at Kate. She seemed like a different person all of a sudden. She had everything she wanted: she was the captain of the cheerleading squad now, the most popular girl in school. But she looked anxious, depressed even. She'd lost weight, she had dark circles under her eyes, and no amount of makeup could cover them. Being on top was hard work—especially at a school like ours—and I guess she was learning that.

"I've got to go back to Mill's," I said, turning around. I'd grab a lemonade there instead—I wasn't in the mood to hang out with Julian.

But he took my arm and pulled me closer. "Is something wrong?"

"No," I said simply, shaking him off.

"Come on, Kam. We know each other..."

Did we, though? "Did you have fun at the party at *your* house?" I asked.

Julian was surprised at first but then tried to shrug it off. "I didn't organize it, Kam, my sister did."

"Yeah, but you sure looked like you were having fun with all those people you like to call assholes."

"There was alcohol there and music; what do you expect? I mean, your boyfriend was there too!"

Taylor? Taylor had gone to the party? "Taylor…"

"He was like the first guy to show up, and I'm sorry to tell you this, but he was flirting with Ellie all night."

"Stop lying, Julian!" I was pissed now, and I turned my back to him. "You always say what great friends we are. But you don't think twice about how something you say might hurt my feelings. One minute you're all like *Oh God, I can't stand our classmates*, and the next minute you're partying with them. Whatever. I don't care, I've got to go to work."

He hurried around to face me. "You don't realize this, Kam, but you're the one who pushes everyone away. Why do you think Taylor was there last night? Because you just left, and you didn't even tell him where you were! He asked me how you got home, and I had no idea what he was talking about! Why do you lie to people? You'd rather walk home than get a ride from your boyfriend, and then you say I'm the one who hurts people. So I tell you things you don't want to hear—but have you ever considered maybe you need that? That you need someone to knock you off your pedestal?"

I was shocked by what he was saying, and I wasn't in the mood to put up with anyone's bullshit. "I didn't make that fucking pedestal, Julian! Everyone else put me on it! And you know why? Because they're all so fucking lame that they need someone to follow so they can feel good about themselves! *Did you see what Kami's wearing today? Did you hear where Kami went on vacation? Did you see Kami got a bike? I think I'm gonna get one too! Did Kami cut her hair? Why isn't Kami smiling? Why isn't Kami going out with Danny anymore? Why isn't Kami dressing like she used to? Where's Kami's car? Let's all bully Kami because she's not giving us enough attention, and we're all just a bunch of dickheads anyway!*"

Julian seemed shocked by my outburst, but his expression then changed to what looked like admiration. "You're right," he said, taking a deep breath. "I agree with you. They're all living in a stupid bubble, and all they care about is what other people think. You're not like that, and that's why I like you, Kam. That's why as soon as I met you, I knew you were special. You've got an aura, and it made me want to get to know you."

"There's no such thing as auras, Julian."

He clutched my cheeks so tightly I wanted to pull away. "They exist. And you have one. And if other people can't see it, then fuck them."

I inhaled deeply and took two steps back. I wasn't in the mood to have that conversation. Not with anyone, and especially not with him. No matter what he said, he'd been at that party, he'd enjoyed it, and he hadn't thought of inviting me. Even though it was in his own home! "I gotta go back to work," I said.

"I'll see you at the bonfires, though, right?"

"I don't know."

When all the cakes and brownies and muffins and pies were done, Mrs. Mill let me go home. It was five in the afternoon by then. On my way, I realized I was no longer excited by what had once been one of my favorite celebrations. I missed my friends. I missed Ellie, who was a lost cause. Every time I saw her, she gave me mixed signals. I missed Kate. Yes, even Kate. Despite everything, we'd always gotten along. I sure as hell missed my dad. He had loved the Bonfire Fest and always made an effort to attend. He loved telling us stories when we were gathered around the fire. I remembered how my brother used to fall asleep and Dad would take him home, and then I'd stay late talking with my friends.

Dad and I hadn't talked since he'd left. It was no surprise. He was affectionate when he was around, but he'd never been good about getting in touch when he was off on his business trips, and I knew it would be hard for him to start now.

I was in my room changing when my grandmother shouted, "Kamila, come down here right now!" from what I assumed was the living room. I pulled on my skinny jeans and favorite wool sweater, and laced up my black snow boots: the ideal outfit for enjoying a bonfire in the snow.

I wasn't sure who I would go with. Taylor hadn't messaged me since yesterday, and Julian seemed to think I was pushing him away. *Why is everything in my life so fucked up?* I asked myself. My grandmother was shouting again, and I quickly sent Taylor a message: Where can we meet? I wrote. My grandmother is here, and I need someone to rescue me. I added a smiley face emoji to try to cut through the tension before hurrying downstairs, where I found my mother, my grandmother, and my brother.

After scrutinizing my outfit the same way my mother always did, my grandmother nodded and said, "We're going as a family so people will understand that we're still united. Still strong despite everything." She pushed a beanie cap onto my brother's head.

"It itches," he said, taking it off and throwing it on the ground.

"Cameron!" Mom shouted, scowling at him as she touched up her red lipstick.

"I'm supposed to meet up with friends," I said, putting on my coat.

"Spend some time with us first. You can see them later," Mom asserted.

I didn't want to start a war over it, so I piled into my mother's car with the rest of them and we drove to town. I looked over at the Di Bianco house to see if the brothers' car was there and was bummed to see that it wasn't. Shit... Was Taylor *that* pissed at me?

We parked on a side street near the town square. Even from there, we could hear the music and the crowds.

"Can I get some cotton candy?" my brother asked, excited and pulling Mom's hand.

"Only one," my mother said as she stepped out into the square. My grandmother walked next to her in a pair of tailored slacks and a thick black sweater. She looked impeccable, like my mother, but it was a bit too much for a simple visit to town, I thought.

We walked around for a while, drinking hot chocolate and eating sweets. When we reached the Mill's stall, Mrs. Mill smiled at me and called Cameron over to give him some free treats. My grandmother gave her a serious, haughty look and asked, "Are you the one who hired my granddaughter?"

Mrs. Mill, who was the sweetest person in the world, smiled and said, "Oh, are you Kamila's grandmother? She's such a delight."

"Hmm. You must not know her very well," my grandmother said, disappointed. Fortunately, it had been years since I'd given a damn what she thought. I'd realized long ago that satisfying her was basically impossible.

"Mrs. Mill, can I have one of these cookies too?" my brother asked.

"Of course, dear," she said with a smile, ignoring my grandmother.

We said our goodbyes and strolled awhile longer through town. Everything looked gorgeous. There were stalls all around, a big bonfire in the center of the plaza, and snowplows parked at the edges of the square with big piles of snow beside them. The roofs of the houses and shops were still trimmed in white—it was all so picturesque that it made me want to sit down on a bench and draw, to capture people's smiles, the firelight reflected in the children's eyes, the bitter cold of the ice and the warmth of the flames…

"Kami!" someone called. I turned. Julian again.

I still wasn't sure how I felt after our argument this afternoon, but I knew I wasn't in the mood to introduce Julian to my mom or my grandmother. There was nothing I could do, though. He marched right up with a big smile on his face and kissed me on the cheek before introducing himself to my family.

"Julian Murphy, pleasure to meet y'all."

My mother and grandmother introduced themselves in turn.

"Are you a friend of my granddaughter?" Grandma asked, sizing him up.

"I sure am," he replied.

My mother glanced strangely back and forth between us and asked, "Aren't you Kate's brother?"

Now Julian stopped smiling. "Not by choice, but yeah. She's my stepsister."

"It's been a long time since Kate's come around the house. Are the two of you fighting or something, Kamila?"

This was the first time my mother had taken an interest in my social life since the school year started.

"No," I lied. I didn't feel like telling my mom that Kate and I weren't talking. "I gotta go, all right?" At least Julian was good for one thing—he gave me an excuse to get the hell away from those two women.

"Already?" my brother asked, doe-eyed.

"Just for a little bit, bud. I'll see you soon."

Julian said goodbye, and we walked off in the opposite direction. "The party's at the south bonfire," he said. "I'll take you." He moved to grab my hand, but I resisted.

"I don't want to go anywhere with you, Julian," I said. I hadn't forgotten what he'd said to me, and I wasn't going to pretend I had.

"Why? Because of what I said before? Come on, Kam! It was just a misunderstanding!"

"No, it wasn't, Julian. And stop calling me *Kam*! Thiago is the only one who gets to call me that!" I don't know where that came from, but the words spilled out before I could stop myself.

Julian gave me a strange look, disappointment mixed with something else. "Listen, I'm tired of following you around only to have you treat me this way, *Kam-i-la*. I said I was sorry, but I guess that doesn't matter?"

"You *didn't* say you were sorry, Julian," I responded, wishing he'd just leave me in peace. "You said that I was up on a pedestal. And you said I needed to be knocked off it. Then you said I had a special aura and everyone wanted to be like me. Well, which is it?"

"Do you not see it? You are different. You're special..." He tried to touch me, but I drew back.

"I'm not, goddammit!" I said, starting to lose it. "And you know what? There are times when I miss the way things were before you got here. I know it's not your fault, but this year has been absolute shit, and every day I'm just more and more alone."

"I wonder why that is," he answered sarcastically, apparently without thinking. Then he corrected himself automatically, telling me he was sorry, but the damage was done. And either way, I wasn't in the mood to accept anyone's apology.

"Maybe you're right... Maybe I should be alone," I said, very serious. "And *alone* means without you popping up around every corner to first stroke my ego and then say something that makes me want to crawl into a hole."

"I thought we were friends," he said, but I knew he didn't believe that.

"Friendship is something to be earned. And I've got too much to deal with right now to try to earn anything from anyone. Sorry."

"Kamila!" he shouted as I walked off.

But I wasn't in the mood to talk to him or anyone else.

I wanted to be alone. Truly alone.

CHAPTER FOURTEEN

Kami

EVENTUALLY, I MADE MY WAY TO THE NORTH BONFIRE, WHERE I knew I wouldn't have to see any of my classmates. It was huge, and the reflection of the flames against the white snow was incredible. All I wanted to do was draw!

Since it wasn't that late, I decided to turn around and go to the art supply store downtown, which was ten minutes away, to buy a sketchbook and some pencils. Nothing fancy, but they would do for now. My urge to capture what I saw all around me was just too intense to ignore. On my way back, a few yards from the fire, I found a tree stump: the perfect place to sit down and work.

Taylor hadn't responded to my message. I didn't know if he was angry at me or just hadn't picked up his phone, but I also didn't want to overthink it. Julian had to have been lying when he said Taylor had been flirting with Ellie. I didn't know what the hell he was getting at with that, but if he kept going down that road, he could kiss his so-called friend goodbye forever.

I opened the sketchbook and started drawing. There weren't many people there, just a few families. The north bonfire was more of a calm place, whereas the parties at the south one always devolved into chaos.

As I sketched curves and lines and crosshatched shadows, I let my mind wander, thinking of all the things that had happened over the past few months: Taylor and Thiago coming back to Carsville, my breakup with Danny, my dad's financial problems, the divorce, leaving the cheerleading squad, losing my car, getting a job, Dad moving away, meeting Julian... I stopped for a moment, realizing of all the things on my list Julian was the only good one. I wondered if I'd been too hard on him. He'd overstepped and stuck his nose in plenty of times when he shouldn't have, but he was also always there for me. In fact, he was the only person who had sought me out on that special day to spend time together.

My eyes focused on the flames, their sinuous movements. Finally, I grabbed my phone, thinking I'd call Julian and tell him I was sorry. We could take a walk together, maybe. I also wanted to see if Taylor had written back. That was when I saw all the messages on my notification screen, insults, words no one had ever used with me before:

SLUT.

WHORE.

FUCKING EMBARRASSING.

IMAGINE WHAT YOUR FATHER WOULD THINK.

MY TURN NEXT.

CHECK OUT THE EX-CHEERLEADER...

My heart was racing as I opened my Instagram. Someone had uploaded a video. From my account.

"Oh my God," I said aloud, reflexively covering my mouth. It was a video of me. Naked. In bed. With someone feeling me up and recording me.

"Oh my God," I repeated, wanting to vomit.

You could easily tell it was me. I was unconscious, and someone was touching me all over without my permission. The thought of me being like that, being recorded without knowing it, was horrifying and made me feel ashamed. I stiffened, as though frozen, the only sound was the blood pumping through my veins, almost as if it were trying to rouse me from the state of shock I'd been plunged into. Then I jerked, as if struck by an electric shock. I dropped my phone, crumpled to the ground, and puked next to the stump where I'd been sitting.

"Are you OK?" a stranger asked. But I couldn't manage to say anything back.

I grabbed my phone, wiped my mouth with the back of my hand, and watched the video again. It was short, but it automatically repeated over and over, like a GIF. You could see my face for just a second, long enough for people to know it was me, then the camera moved down to my breasts, which a hand touched and squeezed, that was it.

I'd never let anyone record me like this.

And I'd only ever slept with one guy.

I got up somehow and started walking, unsure what I was doing, with the video playing over and over in my mind. Over and over. I crossed town in record time, or so it seemed, reaching the south bonfire and staring at the crowd through tears. My entire class was there, along with most of the rest of the school, and people were drinking and laughing as they warmed up around the fire.

But I blocked them all out. I saw only one person. The one person I needed to see then.

I walked over to him. Not stopping.

Danny Walker turned around just as my fists flew toward him, taking him by surprise as they landed hard.

"How could you?" I shouted, tears streaming down my cheeks. I was furious as I wiped them away and leaped on him.

I wanted to hurt him. I wanted to see him bleed.

That son of a bitch could have done anything to me, and I didn't even know it. He'd recorded me half naked and put it on the internet for all the world to see.

"Kamila!" someone behind me shouted.

But I didn't care.

I saw a stick on the ground next to the log where everyone had been sitting, all the people who had now stood up and were looking at me, speechless but almost all holding their phones in their hands.

They'd seen it.

Of course they had.

Jesus Christ.

I saw red.

Red.

Red.

Red.

I grabbed the stick and held it up high.

Danny said something, but I couldn't hear him.

All I could see was that video in my head.

Just as I was about to hit him, a strong hand wrapped around my wrist and stopped me.

"Stop!" I heard a voice shout, and someone moved in front of me like a shadow, blocking Danny, who was calling me a crazy bitch.

"You bastard!" I shouted as loud as I could.

Thiago held both my hands and looked into my eyes. "Kam, breathe. What happened? Tell me."

And then, as if I didn't have enough problems already, I had an anxiety attack. I was hyperventilating so badly I thought I would pass out.

"Thiago…" I said, unable to stop the tears.

"It's OK. Just tell me what happened. Please. Breathe, Kamila."

His voice was serious and commanding, and after a few seconds I could feel the air entering my lungs again.

"He recorded me," I said when I finally managed to get a word out. "He recorded me naked and put it on Instagram."

"I didn't record shit," Danny shouted behind Thiago's back. "Maybe you should be more careful who you sleep with if you don't want…"

Those were the last words he got out. Thiago let me go, turned around, took two big steps and punched Danny so hard he fell to the ground.

Blood tinged the snow red.

"I'm gonna kill you," Thiago said in an icy voice that scared me. He hit him again and again. People tried to pull him off, but no one could stop him. Thiago was like a madman. Finally, Julian jumped in. But when he tried to pull Thiago off, he caught an elbow to the lip. I couldn't believe what I was seeing.

Then I remembered that video again.

Those images of my naked body being filmed without my consent. And now that it was on the internet, it would be there forever. I imagined people looking at it on porno sites, anonymous men all over the world touching themselves and gawking at my body, enjoying something that was supposed to be mine.

What was going to happen now?

How could Danny have done this?

Someone must have called the cops because soon we could hear sirens approaching. Everyone took off, leaving their bottles by the fire so they wouldn't get fined for underage drinking. Before I knew it, the police had arrested Danny, Thiago, and Julian, cuffing their hands behind their backs.

"Kam, call my brother!" Thiago shouted. He looked so worried, so scared…for me. As if he wished he could just hold me and make it all better, which is exactly what I needed.

I didn't know what to do. I was alone, and for the first time, I was scared. When the cops pulled away, the few people left were staring at me, probably incapable of believing what I'd done. And of course, they'd all seen the video.

That video would mark a before and after for me. Not even the best hacker in the world would be able to erase it. Little did I know it would cause the death of so many people.

I couldn't see the light at the end of the tunnel. The darkness was approaching and threatening to swallow me up and never let me out again.

For the first time, I needed her. Her. I looked at my phone and dialed.

"Mom," I moaned. "Please come and pick me up."

"It's OK," Mom said, running her fingers through my hair as I lay there crying, arms around her, on the couch. "We'll press charges against him and the school and anyone who's been involved in ruining your reputation. I promise you."

I wiped my face.

"It's not about my reputation," I said.

There was a fire in the fireplace, and Mom, Grandma, and I were in the living room after I asked them to pick me up and told them what had happened.

I remembered all the times Danny had wanted to record me when we hooked up. Obviously, I'd always said no. But that asshole... Had he drugged me so he could record me, or had I just been asleep? I had no idea, and now he'd uploaded the video to ruin my life and humiliate me in front of everyone.

"Are you sure it was Danny Walker?" my mother asked.

"Who else would it be, Mom?"

"Aren't you going out with Taylor Di Bianco?" She pursed her lips.

"Taylor would never do something like that! Are you out of your mind? Jesus... I'm going to go call him. I just realized he has no idea what's happened. He doesn't know where Thiago is or where I am..." When I picked up my phone, I saw ten missed calls and dozens of messages from him. The last one read: If you don't respond within five minutes, I'm coming to your house.

I looked at the time. He had sent it exactly six minutes before. Just as I went to write back, the doorbell echoed through the living room, making us all jump.

"Who the hell is here at this hour?" my grandmother asked, looking offended.

"It's Taylor," I said, getting up.

My mother grabbed my arm.

"I don't know if you hanging out with guys right now is the best idea, Kamila..."

"He's my boyfriend...and he's my best friend too. I need to see him." I pulled my hand away and ran to the door.

When I opened it, he didn't even say a word. He just grabbed me and pulled me into a hug that mended my broken heart, just a little bit. His big arms squeezed me tight, pressing my ear into his chest. The sound of his slow and steady heartbeat soothed the tension in my chest. He was my soothing balm, the remedy for my never-ending pain.

"It's going to be OK," he said. "But you have to tell me everything. And I need to know where my brother is."

CHAPTER FIFTEEN

Thiago

WE WERE TAKEN TO THE CARSVILLE POLICE STATION, WHERE WE were fingerprinted and thrown into a cell. Danny was kept in isolation—I don't know if it was because he was out of control or because they knew who his parents were and wanted to keep him protected. Julian and I were placed in a three-man cell where some guy was already asleep on the grimy bench. It was probably best that way—I might have killed Danny if he had been in there with us, and I let the cops know, even though, as they said, that could be used against me.

Julian barely spoke, which was fine by me. I did apologize for his split lip, but that didn't mean we were friends. All I could think about was Danny Walker. I prayed we'd get bailed out at the same time so I could finish what I'd started. Maybe I'd get locked up again. Who cares. If what Kam had told me was true, if he had made that video and uploaded it, he had to pay, and there was no way he could hide from me forever.

The dirtbag.

I didn't regret what I'd done to him, and I doubted I'd regret anything in the future.

"Is it true about the video?" Julian asked.

Sitting on the floor and staring down, I said, "Yeah."

I didn't like Julian. I wasn't sure why. Was I jealous because Kam seemed to like him so much? I don't know, but I hated him for being so close to her.

"Is there any proof it was Danny, though?"

I looked up and at him. "Kamila said it was him. What more proof do you need?" For the first time in the hour since we'd been in that cell together, I truly paid attention to him. Then something clicked in my head, and the image I had before me suddenly reminded me of something else, something similar. Julian started going on about how he didn't think Danny was capable of such a thing, even though he was an asshole, and how something was going on at school and it seemed like someone had it out for Kam and he was worried about her. How he'd had an argument with her, and it had hurt his feelings and whatever. He wouldn't shut the fuck up, and I just kept staring at him because I was starting to realize something.

"You and I, we've seen each other before," I said, standing up.

Julian trailed off. "What?"

"June thirteenth. Williamsburg. Brooklyn, New York. I beat a guy up, bad. My knuckles were bleeding like crazy. And you were in the cell with me. Just like right now."

I watched Julian closely to see how he reacted.

"You've got the wrong guy," he said, walking to the other side of the room. "I've never been locked up in my life."

Bullshit.

I remembered it like a movie being projected inside my head. I remembered his face, how relaxed he'd been. I remember that because I'd envied him. I had been terrified. I'd beaten a man, and they'd had to take him to the hospital. I'd spoken to a public defender, he'd told me things weren't looking good, I might get felony assault and do real time.

While I was nervous, frightened, cold—reliving the fight over and over in my head—there he was, completely at home. Like he knew he was going to be all right and he was just in there by mistake.

I remember how the cop had walked over and looked at him with disgust, with rage almost, and said, "You got out of it again this time, Jules. But someday, somebody will wipe that smile off your face, kid. I can only hope it's me."

Jules, as he was called then, smiled and stood, dusted off his clothes, and walked out, turning back briefly to wink at me. I'd wanted to jump up and beat his ass, but I didn't. I couldn't afford to make things worse for myself. Coming back to reality, I stared at Julian. No, this wasn't the first time he'd been in jail. Or the second.

"Do I have the wrong guy, Jules?" I asked.

He turned around quickly. I'd caught the fucker. He'd reacted before he could stop himself. And as we stared at each other, I was absolutely certain that out of everyone locked in a cell that day, the only one who should definitely stay there was him.

"My name's Julian," he corrected me. But it was too late. I knew his secret. The only questions were why he had changed his name and what he had done to get locked up the last time.

"Yeah, right," I said. "My mistake." And I sat back down. No reason to show my hand too soon.

The satisfaction of remembering where I knew him from had almost made me forget how angry I was about Danny Walker, but soon the memory of what he'd done came back, and with it my rage. I needed to get my thoughts in order.

"Thiago Di Bianco," a cop called out. "Someone's paid your bail." He took out a key and opened the cell.

"Who?" I asked as I stood.

"I don't know. It's a guy and a girl."

"There's no one for me?" Julian asked.

"No, now stand back as I open the cell."

Julian caught my gaze before sitting back down.

"Hey, dude," I told him, feigning an innocent expression. "Sorry for getting you wrapped up in this. You want me to call someone to…"

"My sister Kate's on her way," he said simply. I nodded and walked out.

The cop guided me down a long hallway into the waiting room. Kam was the only person there. Her loose blond hair shining like always. Her long legs clad in the same jeans she'd worn to the bonfire. I'd been watching her in them from a distance, a drink in my hand, thinking how incredible she looked. She had her sweater hanging over one arm—it was too hot in the police station to wear it. Her white cotton shirt was snug, showing off her tiny breasts. But none of that mattered, only her face. Her precious face swollen from crying, and the worry in her eyes as she saw me.

She hurried over, hesitated for a moment, unsure whether to touch me. I decided for us both, grabbing her hand and pulling her close for a hug.

"Taylor's…"

"I don't care." I cut her off, smelling her hair, her perfume.

My brother deserved better. Of course, he did. I hadn't lied when I said that, when I'd let her know what she was doing to him was wrong. But my real motivation was to get her away from his arms, from his kisses. I wanted her for myself. She and I, we deserved each other. Right? I knew I'd hurt her when I told her I was testing her that time we'd hooked up, but of course, that wasn't the whole story. I knew she wanted me in a way she could never want my brother—some things are just obvious. I was losing the ability to stay away from her, to pretend she didn't matter to me, to deny the attraction I felt for her. And it wasn't just attraction. It was much, much more.

"I see you're all right," Taylor said, cutting short our embrace. I opened my eyes and found myself face-to-face with my brother's tense, cold stare. The atmosphere was uncomfortable, and Kam didn't know which one of us to look at.

"I talked to Perez," he said, taking me by surprise. Part of me had been ready for another possible confrontation, but this time with my own brother. Perez was a hacker. He'd come in handy more than once. What a coincidence it was for Taylor to mention his name, because I'd just been thinking about him on my way out of the cell. Taylor continued: "I told Kami I asked him to look into what was going on with her Instagram. He said he'd try to have something for us in few days, but then when he got back to me, he made one thing clear: This isn't just some regular guy doing this, it's someone who understands firewalls and things like that. Once he's cracked one of your passwords, he's in. It's not just someone fucking around. If he's hacked Kami's phone, he could have all kinds of other information about her. For now, Perez hasn't got much more for us."

"I already told you guys, it's Danny. He's the one behind this," Kami said, hugging herself.

A cop came over and clapped my brother on the back with a smile. It took me a few seconds to recognize him.

"I heard you boys were back, but I sure as heck didn't think I'd see you here," he said. *Milo*, his name tag read. It was the same cop who had driven us home when my sister Lucy died in the accident on the bridge eight years before. Seeing him again made my heart ache. But he had been good to us, the father figure we needed when our parents went to the hospital with my sister, when they couldn't be there for us because their grief was too great.

I couldn't believe I'd forgotten his name, but I guess when you have a traumatic experience like that, you suppress the details because you don't want to ever relive them again. Taylor must have felt the same as I did because he looked a little confused as well.

"How's it going, Milo?" I asked, shaking his hand. Taylor followed suit.

"I hear y'all got in a fight?" he said, looking at me.

"Something like that." I responded as Milo's eyes glanced down at my bloody knuckles.

It looked worse than it was—I hadn't had a chance to wash my hands, which were caked with dried blood, my shirt was torn, and there was dirt and blood on my pants and in my hair.

"I see." He frowned.

"Sir, he was defending me," Kami said.

"I know." The cop looked at her. "I'm going to have a word with the sheriff, and we're going to see if we can't just pretend this never happened. No promises, though."

I had to fill out some paperwork while Kam and my brother waited outside. One look was enough to tell how tense they both were. My brother looked like he wanted to smash something with his bare hands. When I was done, I walked straight up to Kam. Staring into her swollen eyes, I couldn't forget for a second why we were there. "You should press charges," I said.

"I don't want to," she answered. I could tell from her tone that my brother had already been trying to convince her of this.

"Why not?" I asked. "What he did is a crime. It's sexual assault and an invasion of privacy. People can't get away with that shit anymore. You need to file a report." I tried to sound relaxed, hoping to be more persuasive that way.

"I just want to forget all this ever happened and go to bed."

"Kam…"

"Kami..."

My brother and I had spoken her name at the same time.

"I appreciate everything you guys are doing, I really do," she said, looking back and forth between us. "But there's no way to prove it was Danny, and I don't feel like starting a war and suffering more than I already have."

"You're wrong, though," I said, taking a step toward her. I stopped myself from grabbing her hands since my brother was there. "If you don't turn him in now, it may never stop."

"I don't want to get the courts involved, really." She brushed her hair back from her face and sighed deeply. "Right now, I just need to get some rest. I don't want to think about this shit anymore. Please."

My brother started to say something, but just then the door opened, and we turned to see Kate. She was clearly nervous, but she forced a smile.

"I see you got out," she told me.

"Yeah. Julian's waiting for you." I watched her closely.

She didn't betray anything as she looked over at Kam. "Kami, I'm so sorry about what happened." She seemed sincere. "I just want to tell you, I'll never speak another word to Danny again, and neither will the rest of the girls. What he did is unforgivable."

Kam blinked a few times, surprised, and nodded. "Thank you, Kate. Are you all right?" She had clearly noticed Kate's sunken eyes. She didn't look right, and she wasn't even wearing makeup, which was strange for her since she always went around caked in the stuff.

"Yeah, of course," she said, forcing a smile on us. Who was she trying to fool? "High school sure is getting crazy, right?"

"More like people from school," Kam responded curtly.

Kate nodded and pointed at the counter. "I should go ahead and pay my brother's bail."

"How is he, speaking of?" Kam asked, looking at me.

"Good." I answered coldly, unable to help it.

Kate looked at me with an odd expression, trying to figure out what was behind my tone. After all, Julian had been the one to pull me away from Danny.

"We're going to go," Taylor announced. "Do you guys need a ride or anything?"

"No," Kate replied, "I drove here."

I got behind the wheel, my brother sat next to me, and Kam got in the back. I glanced at her in the rearview mirror. No one said anything on the twenty-minute drive home. When I parked and got out, I felt like a third wheel. Taylor and Kam were looking at me strangely. And all I could think about was how she should have been with me. She should have been going up to my room so I could console her, take care of her, caress her until she fell asleep in my arms.

Kam was mine.

Not his.

"Good night," I said, keeping my eyes on Kam another second.

Once I was in my room, the first thing I did was dial a number I knew by heart.

"Perez, what's up, dude?" I said, peeking out the window. "I need you to find out whatever you can about Julian Murphy. If that doesn't get you anywhere, try Jules. Jules Murphy. Please. It's urgent."

I told him I owed him one as I said goodbye and watched my brother and Kam enter the house. I heard their footsteps on the stairs, and the sound of the door across the hall being shut.

I was going crazy.

I couldn't stand this much longer.

CHAPTER SIXTEEN

Kami

I WENT WITH TAYLOR TO HIS ROOM. HE WOULDN'T STOP INSIST-
ing, and I just couldn't say no. It seemed wrong knowing that
Thiago was just across the hall, but I needed to be with someone
who could offer me a sense of peace and security, and nobody was
better at that than Taylor.

Even before we'd gone to the station, he had hugged me and
calmed me down. My mother had seen us and had to acknowl-
edge him. Unlike her, Taylor had been polite—even nice—despite
what had happened in the past. That made me love him a little
bit more. He was someone who knew how to put his own issues
aside, especially if it meant making me happy.

And I knew that was something Thiago could never do. He
still blamed my mother for everything—he would never agree to
being in the same room with her. For him, the loss of his sister was
still my family's fault, and that would always come between us, no
matter what he said.

I sat on Taylor's queen-size bed and fell back onto the mattress.
The ceiling was still sprinkled with the glow-in-the-dark stars I'd
given him one year for his birthday. "Remember how hard it was
to stick them up there?" I asked.

"What?" He was taking off his T-shirt and putting on a pair of comfy track pants.

"The stars," I said, pointing up.

"Oh, yeah," he replied, as if he'd forgotten they were there.

"It took us two whole afternoons. Remember, we had a ladder up here and you fell off?" I smiled, admiring his body. He'd come over to sit next to me.

"Do I remember?" he asked, pointing at his front teeth. "Thank God they were my baby teeth."

I couldn't help but laugh. "Lie down with me now, and let's look at the stars," I said softly, and he did. When he turned off the bedside lamp, their yellowish glow was the only thing we could see.

"It's funny how sometimes, as lovely as something might be, we stop noticing because we get used to it, even though it's right in front of our noses." As I said this, I kept thinking about that beautiful spring day when we were kids and something as silly as sticking plastic stars to the ceiling could fill us with happiness.

"Is that what it's like with me, Kami? Have you gotten so used to me that you just look right past me?"

I felt a stab in my heart, and I turned to him.

"Why do you say that, Taylor?"

"I've seen how you look at him," he responded, and I froze. "And he looks at you the same way. Don't deny it, OK? I know there's something between you two."

"Taylor, I..."

"It makes me so mad I want to walk across the hall and kill him, Kami, and he's my brother! After Mom, he's the person I love most in this world. But when I'm with you..."

"Taylor, I love you," I said, grabbing his face and turning it toward mine. But I didn't deny his accusation. And that didn't pass unnoticed.

He shook his head and then looked straight at me.

By then my eyes were used to the darkness, and I could read the feelings on his sweet face. The face I wanted to see as soon as I woke up when I was a little kid, the same face that made me feel so calm, so at home.

"Tell me to love you and I will. No hesitation, no more insecurities," he said, his voice so serious that any other thoughts on my mind disappeared. I was entirely focused on Taylor. "Tell me to love you and I'll follow you anywhere. But first, tell me I'm the only one you want to love you."

My heart started racing. My feelings flew out in every direction, as if I was levitating, and I felt my mind ordering me to clear things up once and for all, to accept what I had, let myself be happy.

The image of Thiago flashed in my mind. I loved him too, but we'd never be happy. I could never be happy with someone who hated my family. Someone who still blamed me, in part, for his sister's death. The brother of someone else I loved. My boyfriend, Taylor.

If things ended with Taylor, they would end with Thiago. That was an undeniable fact. I couldn't just be with one and then the other, trying them on like outfits. That wouldn't work, and I could never forgive myself for doing it.

Was it selfish to stay with one because I didn't want to lose both?

Was it selfish to give Taylor a chance when my heart was divided and I could never stop feeling what I felt for his brother? Was it selfish to love him so much and love another person the same or more? Was it selfish that it didn't matter to me because I needed him by my side?

Yes, it was. And yet I whispered his name, "Love me, Taylor." I brought my lips close to his and said, "Love me because you're the only person who knows how."

For a moment, we held back, inhaling each other's breath, and I could sense all the contradictions in his head. It wasn't easy for him to ignore everything he saw between his brother and me.

I promised myself I would never again show any emotion for Thiago. I would keep my feelings to myself. It was Taylor who deserved me, who deserved my love, my affection...I slid on top of him. He could read the intention in my eyes.

"Kami, I don't know if this is a good idea, if we should really..."

But I kissed him before he could say any more. "You're the only one I want and need right now." I caressed his face.

"But who will you need tomorrow?"

"Tomorrow I'll need you more than today," I said, sweeping my fingers down his cheeks to his bare chest.

"Are you sure?"

There was sorrow in his words, and I said nothing more. I decided from then on I would try to *make him* happy. I wouldn't tolerate hearing sadness in his voice. I kissed his bare skin, running my tongue down his abs—abs only a guy who worked out every day could have. I ran my hands over his body, and he was touching me now too, in a way I could tell he had been wanting to do for so long.

We hadn't done it yet because we hadn't found the perfect moment. But sleeping with Taylor was something I'd been looking forward to, even if I hadn't thought I'd be capable of it until now. The fact that the last person I'd been with had violated my privacy and broke my confidence hurt so much that I needed to do something to remedy it.

Taylor didn't let me toy with him for long. Before I knew it, he'd grabbed me by the waist and flipped me over, getting on top of me. He pressed his hard dick between my legs, seeking me out desperately. We didn't speak. It was a game of looks and caresses.

The oldest game in the world, played out with the sweetest, kindest person I'd ever known.

I slipped my clothes off slowly as he kissed my bare skin until suddenly I couldn't take it anymore. "Please," I urged. Meanwhile he was still fully dressed from the waist down.

"I want to taste you first," he said, kissing his way down my stomach. He tugged my panties off and slowly licked me... I squirmed shyly with pleasure. "I'm going to devour you," he said. Feeling his breath between my legs, I felt a wave of immense pleasure and I couldn't wait for it to crash over me.

When he finally tasted me, he didn't stop until I was trembling against his lips, my wetness mixed with his saliva, and I finally knew: This was what it meant to trust someone. This was what it meant to be together.

This was what sex was supposed to be like.

I should never have given my virginity away before I was ready. We have this idea that sex is just sex and we shouldn't make such a big deal about our first time. Like if my friends are doing it, doesn't that mean I should do it too? If my boyfriend wants to, then why not? We treat it like it's nothing, but it matters. Sex is more than just taking off your clothes, touching each other, having an orgasm. Sex is complicity, trust, emotion—or at least it should be. And it should be every time we do it. From the first to the last. Losing your virginity to some asshole is something that can mark you for life.

That video proved it.

With Taylor touching me, I felt comfortable. I felt desired. With Taylor kissing my mouth, my thighs. With Taylor unable to resist the urge to finger me. Slowly at first and then fast, so fast I couldn't keep from moaning. Moaning from pleasure. I was on the verge of coming when Taylor pulled back and opened the drawer in his nightstand. "I want you to come with me inside you," he said, kneeling next to me with the condom in his hand. "But first, will you put it in your mouth, please…" He was practically begging.

And I did. I took him in my mouth, making him quiver. I tasted him, and my mind…dammit, why did my mind do this to me? How could I be comparing the two of them? But I was. I won't tell you who was longer, or thicker, just that they had both been gifted with good genes—the Di Bianco brothers were well-endowed…

I'd never minded giving blow jobs. It's not like I had a lot of practice, but I'd gone down on Danny more than a few times and, well, it was something I felt comfortable doing. I liked feeling in control, like I could pleasure someone with my lips.

"Jesus, Kami," Taylor said, tipping his head back as he sighed from pleasure. I could have kept going until he came, but he stopped me and stared at me with his eyes full of lust.

"You put it on me," he said, handing me the condom.

I did it carefully, remembering how they'd taught us in Sex Ed, pinching the tip as I rolled it all the way down, being careful not to tear it with my fingernails.

Taylor sighed, and I could feel my insides trembling as I anticipated having him inside me. He got on top of me and kissed my neck, my breasts, my face, my ears. I could feel the tip of his penis graze my labia, and I parted my legs to let him in. I'd thought I'd be nervous, but no: my body was relaxed, ready to savor every kiss and caress.

"You're so pretty, Kami," Taylor said, looking down at me. Then he entered me, carefully but firmly.

I arched my back. He didn't stop until he was all the way in.

"Oh my God," I moaned, exhaling deeply as I got used to the feeling of him inside me. He began to move, slowly, watching my reaction to make sure he wasn't hurting me. Once he could see I liked it and my body was rocking in time, he thrust harder and faster. I gasped, yelped with pleasure.

"Oh, fuck, Kami…" he said, speeding up still more.

I didn't want to come yet, not so quickly. I pushed him aside and straddled him so I could be in control. In that position, it was easier to touch myself as I rode him. He held my waist and matched my rhythm, guiding me up and down faster and faster.

"I'm going to come," he said after we'd been at it a while. I was riding him hard, and I never wanted it to end. I knew he was holding out as long as he could so that I could climax first.

I leaned over him, pressing our chests together in search of his mouth, and he pulled me into a deep kiss. Then he grabbed my hips frantically. The headboard was pounding against the wall, but we hardly noticed. All I wanted was to feel his pleasure, to experience his orgasm as he clutched me.

And when he came the sounds he made filled me with joy.

"Holy shit," he said, squeezing me tightly.

I knew I might not come that first time. Taylor would need to learn how to touch me. And I would have to teach him what I liked and didn't—I'd have to learn for myself what I wanted out of sex. I didn't have much experience. So I was surprised when he came back for me after tossing the condom in the trash, leaning over me as he opened my legs, eyes wide with desire for more.

"What are you doing?" I asked.

"What do you mean, what am I doing? You didn't come yet," he said, kissing my thighs.

That was the word I wanted to hear: *yet*. He didn't lie down and fall asleep with a quick kiss good night. He didn't go immediately into the shower just to come out saying, *You know, it's getting late…*

Instead, he said, "Relax. It's your turn now."

And he didn't stop until he'd memorized the first chapters in the manual of my desire. He didn't stop until he'd learned what I liked and what I didn't, how fast to go, how much I could take, how long to leave me hanging.

He didn't stop until he could see I was enjoying it.

And with that, he took with him all I had left to give.

It was around six in the morning when I opened my eyes. I didn't really know where I was at first, but then I saw the stars on the ceiling. I looked at my watch. If Mom had gotten up already and found my room empty, there wasn't much I could do to avoid punishment.

Looking at Taylor, I remembered the night we'd spent together. I felt butterflies in my stomach and couldn't stop myself from smiling. And why would I? So many bad things had happened, and here was something so good with Taylor. We were closer than ever. And I had needed that to move on, to leave behind...

My mind froze, and I gathered my things as best as I could. I had fallen asleep in one of Taylor's T-shirts, which I took off and folded carefully, leaving it on his bed. Once I was dressed, I stepped out into the hall. And as soon as I closed the door, the one across from me opened before I had time to run or hide.

Thiago was there, shirtless, looking forlorn, wounded, and incredulous. I didn't know what to say or do. I stood motionless with my wool sweater in my hands, staring at the very person I didn't want to see that morning.

Thiago pursed his lips, and in his green eyes I could see him struggling with his feelings as his mind tied together loose ends and tried to grasp what all this meant. He seemed to be asking me, *How could you do this?* I thought he would walk past me, go do whatever he had opened the door to do, but instead he reached out, pulled me into his room, shut the door, and pressed me against it. Not only did I not have time to stop him—I didn't even have time to think.

"You're mine, understand," he said, cupping my cheeks in his hands. "You're mine, and I'm yours, dammit!"

His lips pressed against my mouth, and at first I wanted to stop him, but I melted when his tongue touched mine and his hands slid down to grip my waist. I felt myself melting. Shit! The explosion of feelings made me tremble against my will! No! I told myself: No, no, no. Not again. I pushed him gently, and I was sure he felt it because he hesitated. I pushed him again, this time harder, and he pulled away, turning his head so I couldn't see his reaction.

"I can't do this, Thiago," I said, feeling at last that I'd made a decision. Taylor loved me, and I loved him. I had decided to give him everything. And I wasn't going to deceive him anymore. Thiago and I were finished.

When he turned back, I could see the pain in his eyes. But there was something else there. Something uglier. "We both know you're making a mistake," he said, trying to control his voice. "You have feelings for me. It doesn't matter how much you try to deny it. And even if I wish I didn't have them for you, I do. As long as I can remember, you've been stuck in my head. Ever since you used to wear those pigtails, and I'd pull on them just to piss you off. I always wanted your attention. Why the hell do you think I picked on you so much when we were kids? I'd see you running to Taylor to defend you or protect you, knowing I'd do it better than he ever could."

"Thiago, that was a long time ago," I said, trying to steady my voice.

"You think things are any different now? That I couldn't take better care of you than anyone?"

"Thiago, you're the one who told me we couldn't be together," I reminded him, trying not to let my voice betray how fragile I was feeling.

"I changed my mind, OK!" he said loudly, taking a step toward me. "I can't see you with him. I can't stand it. I feel like I'm burning inside when I think about the two of you alone together."

I'd never seen Thiago like this before. Never. He had always tried to hide his feelings. Had always played tough, like nothing got to him, no matter how hard anyone tried.

"I've got to go," I said as he stepped so close to me that I felt like I'd die if I didn't kiss him or hug him or do something to ease his pain.

"You don't, though. You're going because you don't have what it takes to admit you feel the same way I do."

"No, I don't! I love your brother," I said, lowering my tone.

"You can tell yourself that as many times as you like, but you secretly know I'm the one you want."

"You're wrong," I said through clenched teeth.

"Fine, I'm wrong," he responded, throwing his hands up in defeat. "I'm not going to keep trying to convince you. I told you what I wanted to say days ago, the same thing I always think when I see you…"

"And what is that?" I couldn't help but ask. He drew a breath and looked straight through me.

"If you were with me, you wouldn't walk around with that sad look in your eyes. If you were with me, whoever the hell was trying to hurt you would have stopped, or they'd be fucking dead. Admit it: You picked the wrong brother."

"That isn't fair."

"You're right, it's not," he countered. "But life isn't fair. And I'm tired of letting everyone around me take the things that should rightfully be mine."

"You're only saying this now because you know I'm with him. Before, you wouldn't give me the time of day. If you even noticed me, it was only to scream at me and hurt my feelings. Or have you forgotten the way you treated me up until a month ago?"

"I wasn't ready then to accept what I feel for you. What I've always felt for you."

"And now you are?"

"Now I am." His voice was softer as he reached up and tucked a strand of hair behind my ear. "Now I am," he repeated, and I flinched as his fingers grazed my cheek.

"Stop it."

"I can't." But he did. He drew his hand away and let it fall to his side, taking a step back, looking at me with grief, with sorrow, but then with such anger that everything else disappeared.

"I made a decision yesterday, and I'm not going back on it," I said.

"Then get out."

He didn't have to say it twice.

CHAPTER SEVENTEEN

Thiago

I LET HER GO.

I'd said what I had to say. She chose him over me, no matter how much I wished it were the other way around.

Even though I was pissed and hurt, that didn't stop me from answering the phone a few minutes after Kam walked out of my room. It was Perez. And he didn't have good news.

"What's goin' on, man," he said, sounding wired, as if he'd been up all night. And knowing him, that was likely—he'd either been up playing video games or looking into what I'd asked him about the night before.

"Hey, man. Did you find anything out?" I asked, sitting down on the swivel chair at my desk and looking through the window to be sure Kam made it home safe and sound. After a second, her light came on and I was able to relax. I didn't like the way things were going at school, not to mention that repugnant video Danny Walker had put on the internet...

"Yeah, that's why I'm calling. So the name Julian Murphy was basically a dead end. A couple of social media accounts, none of them more than a few months old. Jules Murphy, though, that's a different story." He sounded serious.

"What'd you find?" I sat up and paid close attention.

"I got his school records. It's weird, though—he never stays anywhere for long. Two years, tops. He was at one place in Brooklyn. His grades suck, his disciplinary record is shit too, he's been kicked out of a few places for fighting. He's been changing schools like that since he was fourteen."

"Getting expelled?" I asked.

"No, he left of his own accord. So I kept investigating. I checked the records of different police departments around New York, and you wouldn't believe…"

"What…?" I started to get a really bad feeling.

"He's been arrested a bunch of times. But it never came to anything. They always decide to drop the charges."

"What kind of charges are we talking?"

In the second of silence afterward, I looked back over at Kam's window.

"Stalking," Perez said calmly.

"Stalking?" I asked. And things suddenly started making sense, even if I didn't like where they were leading me.

"And that's not all." Now I was getting really nervous. "I found this page where he uploads all this weird shit about gay people."

"Yeah, he's gay," I said, remembering that detail.

Perez laughed. "I don't think so, man. It's all batshit homophobic stuff."

"What?" I couldn't believe what I was hearing. "Can you send me the link?"

The message came through immediately, and I clicked on it. It was dark shit for real, with all kinds of nasty stuff—thumbnails and videos of people beating up and tormenting gay kids. And there was a banner at the top of the page that said: *Homosexuality is an abomination and must be punished.*

Everything I saw there was so backward and disgusting, I had to close it after just a few seconds.

"I don't get something, though," I told Perez. "If this dude's so homophobic, why does he go around telling everyone he's gay?"

"He's sick in the head, man. It's impossible to tell what people like that are thinking, but looking at his arrest record, the way he's stalked people in the past, my guess is he's faking it to try to look harmless so he can get close to someone."

I thought of Kam. Fuck, that goddamn psychopath was crazy about her. "Perez, man. I owe you. Seriously," I said, with a sinking feeling inside. I didn't like what I'd just learned, and I was starting to ask myself if Julian wasn't behind all the weird stuff that had been happening at school. "If you find anything else…"

"What I can't help but wonder, though, is why all those girls dropped the charges," Perez said to himself out loud.

"Is there a way to find out?"

"Not unless you ask them directly."

"Have you got any names?"

"Gimme a sec." I could hear the clicking of Perez's keyboard. "I'll need some time, but I might be able to get you something."

"I've got my phone on me twenty-four seven. Just call."

"I'll do that. Oh, and tell your brother I'm still trying to find out who hacked his girl's phone."

I looked back out the window. "She thinks it's her ex, a guy named Danny Walker."

"Danny Walker?" Perez said. "I'm just writing that down because Tay didn't mention him. He goes to the same school, right?"

"Yeah."

"A name always helps, you know. Maybe I can find other traces of him online. I told your brother whoever did this isn't stupid, they know what they're doing."

That didn't add up. Danny Walker, a computer genius? I couldn't see it. There was something fishy about this whole story, and I was starting to doubt whether Danny had anything to do with that video. "Perez," I said, "do you think Jules could be involved in that too?" I was starting to feel sick to my stomach.

"Dude... That video was made in a bedroom.... If what you're telling me is true and Julian or Jules—or whatever his name—is just friends with that girl... Are he and Walker friends? Maybe they're in it together?"

But Julian had stepped into a fight to defend Kam from Danny. It just didn't make sense.

"I don't think so," I said, but I wasn't sure. "I don't know whether to connect Julian's history as a stalker with all the stuff that's been happening to Kam... He might be a sicko, but they seem to actually be friends. He's always treated her nicely."

"It's high school, man, who can say. Bullying, revenge porn, that's the kind of thing that goes on nowadays."

"Yeah. It's fucked up. I'm going to get to the bottom of it, though."

"Cool, man, well, I'll be in touch with whatever I find," Perez said and hung up.

I didn't like this.

I didn't like it one bit.

I took a shower, my head so full of confusion I thought it might explode. My intuition told me this wasn't over and Kam wasn't safe. And I wasn't going to stand back and let something happen to her.

I went downstairs and made some coffee just as my mother was coming home from the night shift. As soon as she saw me, she knew something wasn't right. "What's going on?" she asked, sitting down across from me. Her green eyes were just like mine, but lined with deep circles that looked almost purple on her white skin from the endless hours she was working at the hospital to keep us on our feet.

"I just woke up on the wrong side of the bed, that's all," I said as Taylor came in.

"You always wake up on the wrong side of the bed," he said in a tone that sounded almost taunting.

"Are you trying to be a smartass?" I asked. I wasn't in the mood for this shit, and after knowing Kami had spent the night in his room, I was doing my best not to kill him.

"Hey!" my mother said, grabbing my hand and seeing something I wish she hadn't seen. I drew it back under the table, but it was too late.

"Thiago Di Bianco, let me see that hand right now unless you want me to actually get angry," she said.

Fuck.

I brought my hand out and laid it on the table.

"What is this about?" she said. "Are you getting in fights again?"

"Mom, it's nothing," I said, trying to calm her down. I wasn't in the mood to have to apologize to anyone.

"What do you mean, it's nothing? Your knuckles are raw! Who did you hit, Thiago?"

"Danny Walker," Taylor said, pouring coffee into an ugly pink mug. God, I hated Mom's taste sometimes.

"The mayor's son?" my mother exclaimed. "Have you lost your mind?"

"Everything's under control, believe me." I got up and set my cup in the sink. I wasn't in the mood to listen to her.

"They'll fire you over this!"

"They're not firing anybody. You know why? Because if he even thinks of mentioning any of this, I'll fucking kill him."

My mother looked shocked, and she turned to my brother for some kind of explanation. But Taylor told her coolly, "And if he doesn't, I will."

"What in heaven's name!" My mother stood. She was furious, and the combination of her anger and her tiny frame might have been funny in a different context, but not right now. "Tell me right now what's going on!" she said.

My brother gave her the short version, as I felt myself getting more and more angry. I couldn't stand to hear it again, how half the town had seen Kam naked, how she'd been recorded without her consent...

Kam hadn't wanted to press charges.

But if she wasn't going to do something, I was.

Danny Walker's days at Carsville High were numbered. I was sure about that.

CHAPTER EIGHTEEN

Kami

I DIDN'T WANT TO GO TO SCHOOL. IN FACT, I NEVER WANTED TO set foot inside that building ever again. Call me a coward, call me insecure, tell me to toughen up, but when everything around you starts to feel like a threat... This was the first time I understood what it truly feels like to be *bullied*.

Stuff like this had always been so foreign to me. I'd never understood how kids could kill themselves. I'd never truly believed it until I started to feel like anxiety was chewing me up inside. It made me want to run away, just escape everything. I didn't feel safe. And Danny was the one behind it all. I was sure of it.

Mom came to wake me up. Not that she needed to—I was already at my desk drawing, in such a trance that I hadn't noticed what I was sketching, really.

"I'm going to take you to school today," she said. She was already dressed, and my little brother was holding her hand.

"No need," I said, thinking what a terrible idea it was.

"It's time for me to talk to the principal."

"Absolutely not!" I exclaimed. "Mom, you have to stay out of this!"

"Oh, I have to stay out of it? I'm supposed to just let people bully both my children? Are you aware of what's been happening to Cameron?"

I looked at Cam. He was groggy—the poor thing hated having to get up early.

"Of course I know. They called you and Dad to tell you about it, and you didn't even bother to come in. That's why they called me instead."

"How could you not tell me?"

"Why? It's not like you would have done anything."

"Of course I would have!"

I shook my head. "Your besties' little golden boy Danny Walker is the one behind it. If there's anyone you should be talking to, it's them."

"You're telling me Danny Walker is harassing you *and* encouraging kids to beat up your little brother?"

"Cameron, you tell her," I said. "Tell her who's hitting you."

He blinked. He was so scared he could barely get a word out. "I can't."

My mother seemed unable to believe what she was hearing. "What do you mean you can't? You better tell me right now!" she shrieked.

"What's all this shouting?" my grandmother asked from the hallway. She was still in her bathrobe and matching silk pajamas.

"Mom just found out that both her kids are getting harassed at school," I said flatly, although deep down I still didn't see myself as a victim. Where had all my strength gone? I'd always considered myself to be so confident. Until Danny and I broke up, at least. That was where everything had gone wrong. How had I been so blind not to realize he was the one behind it? He'd told me loud and clear! He'd enjoy watching me fall, although he'd never been specific.

"Cameron too?" my grandmother asked indignantly. "Anne, why haven't you done something?"

"What do you think I'm trying to do? I was on my way to the principal's office!"

"Mom, this isn't something you can solve by going to the principal!"

Just when my mother was about to protest, the doorbell rang. "Who could that be?" Grandma exclaimed, marching downstairs.

"Kamila, get your things and get in the car," Mom ordered me. "I'm not going to say it twice."

I didn't really have an option anyway. Outside, snow still covered the ground, and there was no way I would make it on my bike. I could try to hitch a ride with the Di Biancos, but the way things were with Thiago, even walking would be better.

"Kamila, you've got a friend here!" my grandmother shouted.

As I made it down the final step, I saw Julian had two to-go cups of coffee in his hands. Part of me felt relieved.

"I thought you could use a friend today," he said with a sweet smile, and I couldn't help smiling back as I invited him in.

Mom came down with my brother. "I'm taking Kamila to school today," she said sternly.

After looking at me for a second, Julian murmured, "OK then. I had just thought I would." He didn't know what else to say.

"Mom, let Julian take me, OK?" I asked. "I need to handle this stuff myself."

"Kamila," she objected, "I don't like this one bit."

"Are you just going to let her disobey you like that?" my grandmother asked.

"What do you want me to do, Mother? Force her into the car?" I could see Mom was frustrated, but I could also tell I had won. "Either way, Kamila, I am going to talk to the principal, and there's not a damn thing you can do about it."

I asked Julian to wait, and I went upstairs for my coat and bag.

"Let's go," I said, rushing past my family and slamming the door behind me.

Julian and I looked at each other for a few seconds. "I'm sorry," we both blurted out at the same time, breaking into smiles. So we'd had a fight the day before everything went to shit. It had been stupid—there had been no need for it. I'd started to realize Julian was one of those people who couldn't help saying hurtful things when he was angry. I wasn't that way, but I could forgive it, especially when he'd tried so hard to be there for me.

"Come on," he said, pulling me in for a comforting hug. We got in the car. "How are you?" he asked.

"Bad," I admitted, feeling the warmth from the hot coffee spread through my body. Outside, it was freezing cold.

"Your mother's right, Kami," Julian said after a moment of silence. "You should talk to the principal. You need to turn Danny in. What he did..."

"I don't know... I just want to put all this behind me. He knows we know it's him now—he'll have to stop. But I'll tell you one thing: If my brother shows up at home with so much as a scratch on his face, I'll kill Danny Walker. I swear to you, Julian, I will."

"Kamila, he uploaded a video of you naked onto the internet..."

Those words cut like a knife. I think a part of my brain had tried to make me believe it hadn't really happened. Because if I thought about it, it made me want to vomit.

"I can't talk about that right now, Julian. I need time to absorb it. To really grasp that he was capable of doing that."

Five minutes later, we were in the parking lot at school. Right away, I noticed people turning toward me. I could feel the weight of their stares. They weren't looking at *me*, they were seeing that naked body they'd viewed online.

I didn't see him coming. I didn't see him because he came out of nowhere. But then, there he was, grabbing my hands—touching me!

"Please, Kami. You've got to believe me. It wasn't me!"

"Get outta here!" Julian shouted, pushing him away, before I could even react.

Danny tripped and almost fell backward. He looked horrible. The beating Thiago had given him had left him looking disfigured. Both his eyes were black and swollen, and his lip was split. "I need to talk to her!" Danny insisted, looking at me with pleading eyes. I'd never seen him so desperate. "I would never do anything like that! How could you even think that?"

"Don't come near me," I said, feeling the hatred inside me grow. But did I truly hate him? Could I?

"Kamila, your mother called the cops on me! Fucking A, you're going to ruin my future!"

"Hey!" someone yelled behind me, and I heard the slamming of two car doors.

"Get the fuck away from her!" Taylor shouted. Thiago didn't say a word. But his eyes clouded over.

Shit. This was going to end badly. Really badly.

Danny raised his hands in surrender and started walking backward. "Kamila, you know me. You know I wouldn't do something like that." He looked me straight in the eye.

"That's the sad thing," I said, tears in my eyes. "It turns out you would."

The principal appeared. "What's going on out here?" he demanded.

We all turned to him. His presence was at once frightening and a relief. I looked at Thiago. He seemed more relaxed knowing now he'd have to keep his hands off Danny.

"Everyone, get to class. Right now!" The students who had been standing around us dispersed. I couldn't believe the crowd a fight could draw; in a matter of seconds everyone had come to watch. All that was missing was the popcorn.

"Walker and Hamilton, come to my office," he shouted. "As for the rest of you, stay out of my sight."

Holy fucking shit.

Thiago was still staring Danny down.

"I'm not leaving Kami with that creep," Taylor said, walking up beside me.

"Di Bianco, I'm not going to repeat myself. Get to class!"

"No," Taylor replied, and the principal's face turned even redder.

"Di Bianco, either you leave now or you'll have a week's detention."

"Can Thiago come?" I asked.

I didn't want to be alone with Danny either. I barely trusted anyone right now, and certainly not him. Besides, everyone knew he was in a class of his own because he was the mayor's kid. If he was going to try to weasel out of this using his parents' reputation, I wanted to be sure there was a witness.

"Well, I need to talk to him anyway; yes, he can come," the principal grumbled.

I looked back at Julian, who asked if I was going to be all right. I nodded, and Taylor grabbed my hand. "When you're done," he said, "let's get out of here." He gave me a hug in front of everyone.

Pressed against his chest I could smell his cologne, and it made me smile.

"I don't want you to get into trouble because of me. Things are bad enough for all of us already, don't you think?"

"I couldn't care less. You're all that matters to me," he said, drawing me back into his arms and kissing me.

"Get to class now," Principal Harrison repeated.

Taylor and Julian walked off together. Danny, Thiago, Principal Harrison, and I headed toward the office. I had no idea what was coming next. Once inside, I saw Lowell and Kelly Walker, Danny's parents, looking at me like the embodiment of their worst nightmares. To think just a few months before, their dream had been for me to marry their son...

"So, now that we're all here together..." the principal said, sitting at his desk.

"My mother isn't here," I said, regretting the moment I told her not to come. I was being ambushed.

"Tell your mother my door is open whenever she'd like to stop in," Harrison responded. "But I can't just wait around for her—we have a problem that needs to be dealt with immediately."

Danny's mother began: "My son didn't upload any pornographic content to any website." She was equal parts indignant and anxious.

"Pornographic content?" Thiago shouted from behind me, then stepped forward to face Kelly Walker. "Your son filmed Kamila without her permission. That's sexual assault, far worse than mere pornography."

"Di Bianco!" the principal shouted.

"I didn't do it!" Danny screamed.

"Danny, stop lying," I said, feeling insulted. "You're the only person who could have taken that video. You were my boyfriend!"

Danny laughed. "And how many boyfriends do you have now, Kamila? Because I feel like every time I turn around, you're flirting with someone new—"

"Mr. Walker!" the principal stopped him.

Thiago took a step forward, and my hand flew up to grab his wrist. I couldn't let him do it; he couldn't hit him again. Danny looked scared and took a step back.

"What you just said shows how immature, sexist, and idiotic you actually are, Danny," I said, glaring at him.

"Miss Hamilton!" Principal Harrison admonished me.

Now Mr. Walker spoke up: "I will not have my son accused of something this serious without proof. He is a good student, an elite athlete—"

Thiago cut him off with a bitter laugh. "Your son is a fucking drug addict who's only on the team because you're as rich as you are shameless and you were able to pressure this school into not expelling him."

"Mr. Di Bianco, you can leave now!"

"Thiago's staying," I said, standing and leaning over Danny and his parents. "Your son has been harassing me. Not just me, but my little brother. Momo? Are you serious? You actually think that's funny? Scaring little kids? You're despicable!"

Danny looked at me as though I were speaking a foreign language. "Sorry, but what the hell are you talking about?" he asked.

"Stop pretending you don't know!"

"This young lady is clearly losing it," Danny's mother said. "What happened to you, Kamila? You used to be so sweet, so polite, so..."

"Stupid?" I fired back. "To think I lost two years of my life with your idiot son. It makes me want to pull my eyelashes out."

Mrs. Walker was stunned, and despite how upset I was, I couldn't help but enjoy watching her blush at my words. A knock came at the door, and the secretary, looking almost frightened, tried to announce over the shouting, "Mr. Harrison, Kamila Hamilton's mother is out here and would like to speak with you."

My mother, my brother, and my grandmother entered the office. At this point, there was barely room for another soul in there. Harrison slumped in his seat, unable to believe what was happening. Thiago tensed up again. I knew he couldn't stand to be in the same room with my mother, and the tension made me want to scream.

"Let me get this straight," Mom said. "You call a meeting about the harassment my children are both suffering and you don't have the decency to inform me?"

This was the first time in my life I'd seen her take her role as a mother seriously.

"Mrs. Hamilton, I didn't call any meeting. Mr. Walker's parents came to the school…"

"If my daughter is being discussed, I should be part of the conversation," she clipped.

"You should be ashamed of yourself," my grandmother said, looking at Danny and shaking her head.

"Hey," Danny said to my brother, who looked thoroughly lost. "Did I ever do anything to you?"

Cameron hid behind my mother's skirt.

"Leave my brother alone," I said, instinctively taking a step in his direction. "Cam, who's been hitting you at school?"

Cameron looked from me to my mom. "Cam, tell us, please," she insisted.

"But, Momo…" he said, almost crying.

I looked at the principal and Danny's parents.

"I'm sorry, who is this Momo?" Mr. Harrison asked.

"Momo's a creepy doll that scares kids on YouTube and sends threatening messages," Thiago said. "But Cameron, listen to me. Momo doesn't exist." His voice was gentle.

"Cameron, who's been hitting you?" the principal asked.

My brother scanned the room. "George Walker," he finally confessed.

"That's impossible!" Danny's mom said, drawing her hand to her mouth.

I looked at Danny, who seemed shocked. How could he be so two-faced?

"But he only does it because Momo tells him to," my brother clarified. Was he actually defending someone who was hurting him?

"It's his older brother who's giving the orders, Cameron," my mother said, looking at Danny with disappointment. "And to think I once thought you were such a catch for my daughter..."

Danny's mother was about to say something, but then the principal stood. "This is getting out of hand," he said. "Videos on the internet, secret messages from a talking doll. I'll tell you what. From now on, we'll have no more cell phones at this school!"

I looked at him in shock.

"That's seriously your solution?" my mother cried. "No cell phones, but you'll let juvenile delinquents wander the hallways?"

"Mrs. Hamilton, it's not my job to raise your kids for you. As far as I know, there isn't any proof that Mr. Walker is guilty of uploading that video. My hands are tied. As for George, he'll be suspended for bullying and harassment."

"How dare you!" Danny's father shouted, but the principal ignored him.

"About Momo: We'll have the teachers and counselors talk to the kids about this absurd doll, and I can promise you, there will be a thorough investigation. For now, that's all. Thank you." With this, the principal motioned for us to leave.

Despite their outbursts, I could see Danny's parents were relieved that he hadn't gotten punished. There were still the police to deal with, but without any proof... God, I hated him! I hated that asshole with all my heart. As they all filed out, my mother told me not to worry and that she'd pick me up after class. Then she left with my brother and grandmother. Only Thiago, Harrison, and I stayed behind.

"It doesn't take a genius to look at your bruised knuckles and Danny Walker's face and put two and two together, Mr. Di Bianco," the principal said, making us stop in our tracks. Thiago seemed about to speak, but Harrison stopped him. "But for some reason Mr. Walker didn't say a word about you or about why his face is black-and-blue. Once again, I don't have proof. But when I do, Mr. Di Bianco, don't think I'll hesitate to send you packing. Don't play with fire, kid. Or you're likely to get burned. Now go, both of you."

Harrison sank into his chair and expelled a long breath.

Thiago and I left without exchanging a word. Once out in the deserted hallway, I stopped to thank him for staying with me.

"I'm going to tell you something, Kamila. There's more going on here than you think." So he was back to calling me by my full name. I guess that meant he hated me again.

"Look, I'm tired of trying to understand why these things are happening to me." I hugged myself. "All I want at this point is to graduate and get into college so I can get the hell out of here."

Thiago looked around nervously. I realized he had something else to tell me, but he couldn't figure out how to say it.

"Are you OK?" I asked.

"Watch out for Julian, Kam," he warned me in a serious tone.

Julian? What was that supposed to mean? "Julian's my friend," I said incredulously. Was he honestly getting jealous of Julian now too?

"Kam, for once in your fucking life, listen to me. Watch out for him, and don't believe everything he says."

I shook my head and stepped back. "I'm going to be late for class. I'll see you around."

And though he didn't say another word, the look on Thiago's face haunted me for the rest of the day.

CHAPTER NINETEEN

Taylor

As she walked in, everyone in the room turned away from the teacher to stare at Kami. Her eyes scanned the room until she saw me in the back, where I'd saved a desk for her.

"Come on in, Miss Hamilton," the teacher said, and Kami walked down the row of seats until she got to me.

I couldn't believe what had happened between us just a few hours ago. I couldn't believe we'd finally been together, and I'd finally gotten to feel her the way I'd been wanting to for so long. I'd kissed her, touched her—even been inside her. I'd enjoyed experiencing her sweetness and the passion behind that pretty face. Watching her climax had been a highlight of my eighteen years of life. Knowing I was the one who had taken her to orgasm made me so happy, and all I could think about was doing it again.

I had lost my virginity at fourteen. For some people that might seem early, but it had come at a time in my life when everything else was spiraling downward; nothing around me seemed to be working out. Mom hardly got out of bed because she was so depressed, and that depression meant she picked the most terrible boyfriends, guys that only made her feel worse. My brother started getting into big trouble at school, and even though he always looked out for me and for our mom, he was a ticking time bomb about to explode. I remember his face when he'd come home, always so pissed off at the whole world, and his dark humor spread through the house, although he hardly realized it.

Sex was my escape. Girls noticed me as soon as I hit puberty, and especially once I'd grown taller than six feet. And when you're fourteen and seventeen-year-old girls are throwing themselves at you…it's not easy to resist.

I turned to Kami and said in a low voice, "Tell me they expelled that son of a bitch."

She looked at me and then at the door and—I couldn't believe it—there was Walker coming in as though he had done nothing. I almost got up, but Kami held me back.

"Leave it, babe," she said, "please."

I would've liked to split his damn face open. A tense silence fell over the class; even the teacher stopped talking as he came in. Probably everyone in the school, even the staff, knew what had been going on. After all, a nude video of Kami on the internet, uploaded to her own Instagram account without her consent— was the kind of thing that got around.

"You should be in jail," Julian called out from behind me.

"Mr. Murphy!" the teacher chastised him.

"Unbelievable. We actually just let a suspected sex offender walk around the school like it's no big deal," a girl called out.

Kami looked over at her in silent gratitude. Kami hadn't deserved what had happened to her. She hadn't done anything wrong.

"Suspected?" another girl said. "He drugged her and recorded her! How do we know he hasn't done anything else like that?"

Next to me, Kami was starting to tremble.

"Enough!" the teacher shouted, looking at her.

Just then, Danny stood up. "It wasn't me!" he shouted loud and clear. He looked pale, almost faint. I wished I could wrap my hands around his neck. I didn't care about the consequences. That son of a bitch deserved it.

"It was you! Stop lying!" Kami shouted and walked out of the class, ignoring the teacher, who was calling her name.

I followed her. I followed her because I didn't give a shit, and besides, I was afraid if I stayed there, I'd kill him, and man—I'd really enjoy watching him go down, but I didn't want to end up in jail on his account.

"Kami, wait!" I called out, walking into the girls' bathroom behind her.

"I can't take it anymore!" she cried, leaning against the sink as she broke into tears.

"Babe, please...calm down." I wrapped my arms around her tightly.

"I can't." She was hiccuping and sobbing. "I can't stop thinking about what he might have done to me. I tell myself it's just that video, but what do I know! And everyone's seen me, everyone's seen my..."

"It's OK." I pulled her against my chest. "It's not like the old days. People don't think that shit's funny anymore. You saw how they reacted to Danny. His glory days are over... At least at this school."

Kami pulled away to dry her face. I ran my fingers across her cheeks to help smooth away the tears. It broke my heart to see her like that.

"I love you," I said, looking her in the eyes.

She smiled. "I love you too," she said, taking a deep breath to calm down. "And what we did yesterday..."

"It was incredible." I finished her words.

"It was." She got on her tiptoes and kissed me square on the lips. "I'm sorry I didn't say anything before I left, but I knew my mom would kill me if she didn't find me in my room in the morning…"

"It's fine," I said, tucking a strand of hair behind her ears.

"Kami, are you OK?" came a sweet voice at the bathroom door. A head of frizzy curls appeared; it was Ellie.

Kam wiped away the last of her tears and forced a smile. "I'm OK, Ellie."

"I'm sorry for everything…" she said, looking at me. "You were right about Danny." Ellie stared at the ground. I'd almost forgotten she'd hooked up with him.

"It's all right," Kami said, and before Ellie could say anything more, a voice came over the PA: *Attention, students: This message is to inform you that starting tomorrow, students will be required to turn their cell phones in at the office prior to attending class. There will be no exceptions! Cell phones are not to be used on school grounds outside of extraordinary circumstances and only with the permission of the administration.*

Ellie and I both opened our eyes wide, but Kami seemed unfazed.

"This is bullshit, right?" I asked.

"I wish," Kami said. "He told Danny and me in his office. It's supposed to be an anti-cyberbullying measure."

"Give me a break!" Ellie said, leaning back against a stall door. "As soon as we're out the door, we'll all have our phones back and this shit will keep happening. Doesn't he realize that?"

"At least now I can relax knowing that nobody is looking at naked videos of me while I'm walking down the hall," Kami tried to joke. "And no one can send my brother threatening messages during the school day."

"Your brother has a phone?" Ellie asked.

"It's just for emergencies," Kami replied, rolling her eyes. "My mom insisted on it. Dad was against it."

"What are we going to do without our phones?" I grumbled.

"I guess we'll have to actually talk face-to-face," Ellie said, making me laugh.

"I bet nobody will have the balls to talk shit to me to my face," Kami said. I could tell she didn't think the new cell phone ban was such a bad idea.

We left the bathroom as the bell rang, and everyone walked out of their first class. All they could talk about was their phones.

It's mine. I've got a right to have it on me.

Why the hell can the teachers have theirs if we can't have ours?

We should protest!

I'm going to tell my dad to talk to his lawyer.

And wherever you looked, *every single person* had their phone in their hands, as if afraid someone might come along and grab them from their back pockets. It was kind of sad, thinking that our generation no longer knew how to live without them, but I guess that's how it was. Our phones were an extension of our bodies, always there to check the time, look at our messages, scroll through our photo library...

I heard a girl shout, "Hey, dickhead, what are you going to do now that you can't use your phone to film people without their consent?"

We turned to see Danny headed toward his locker.

The three of us froze. I was surprised by how people had risen up to defend Kami. I didn't have the highest opinion of the population of Carsville, but they really seemed to come together to let the former basketball star know how much they disapproved of him.

And I was there to enjoy watching him fall from grace. Fuck him. Fuck him for real. If people wanted to gang up against that pervert, I was happy to join them.

"Rapist!" another girl shouted, and her friends started in along with her.

"Why don't you just get the fuck out of here?"

That wasn't the end of it. Soon they were circulating a petition to have Danny Walker expelled from school. Kami stayed out of it. She had made it clear that she didn't want to be part of anything. She just wanted to forget what had happened and never talk about it again. But through no fault of her own, she'd become the center of attention again, no longer someone people hated, but a feminist symbol and a concrete reason to fight against sexual harassment at school. I understood her reasons for standing aside, but I admired what these girls wanted to do. Danny Walker shouldn't be allowed to stay at our school.

OK, so there was no proof. True enough. But all the signs pointed at him, and there was nothing I wanted more than to see that bastard go down.

More than anything, people were pissed about the phones. We were supposed to put them in a plastic bag with our first and last names on them, and they were going to be locked up in a special room in the office. The students were furious about having their phones taken away, and they felt there was just one person to blame for it: Danny. So you can imagine the kind of treatment he was in for. Things got worse for him by the second. Hardly anyone would speak to him. Following my lead, the basketball team had turned its back on him too. He deserved to be left out in the cold.

Kami was my girlfriend, after all. Everyone knew it. And all that bullshit between them, talking trash and taking sides, that was over. I was the king of the school now, and Kami was my queen. Anyone who messed with her would have to face the consequences.

One of the people hardest on Danny was Julian. He insulted him every time he saw him, and he was part of the group that ganged up on Danny one day outside school. I would have joined them, but Kami begged me for over half an hour to stay out of it. She didn't like the turn things had taken and said she didn't want to see me stoop to Danny's level. She and Julian had a nasty fight about it, and even Ellie had her say, telling Kami she couldn't expect everyone to just leave Danny alone after what had happened.

Danny ended up in the hospital with a broken arm. And that was when I realized things were starting to spin out of control.

Way, way out of control.

CHAPTER TWENTY

Thiago

IT TOOK A FEW DAYS, BUT FINALLY I GOT THE CALL FROM PEREZ I'd been waiting for. I only had one option if I wanted to find out about Julian's lies, and that was talking with one of the girls who claimed he'd harassed her. There was no evidence as to why they'd all dropped the charges. That was something I'd have to find out for myself.

Kam had ignored my warnings. I knew she wouldn't listen to me—she never did—but I needed her to know Julian wasn't who he seemed to be. He was one hell of an actor; he did everything a real friend would do, worrying about her, checking on her, but it was also uncanny how every time there was an altercation involving her, he just happened to be right around the corner. I could usually trust my instincts, and I wasn't going to ignore them when someone I cared about so much was involved. I needed to get to the bottom of this, even if I had to do it alone, because although my brother didn't trust Julian, his hatred for Danny blinded him to everything else.

I didn't really know what was going on with all the students—I wasn't one of them, and my brother wasn't exactly talkative. He avoided me whenever possible. And so I didn't intervene when they kicked the shit out of Danny. Not that I would have—as far as I was concerned, he deserved it.

I was in PE class with the little kids when Perez called. When I saw it was him, I didn't think twice about taking the call. "I've got something I'm pretty sure you'll be interested in," he said. I could tell by his tone he was satisfied with his work.

"Shoot," I said, keeping one eye on the kids. They were playing dodgeball, and I didn't want to miss anything between Cameron and George. I knew well the way kids would elbow each other or knock each other down and then plead, *I was just playing!*

"I've got the number and address of a girl who called the cops on Jules last year," he said. "It wasn't easy, but a guy I know has an acquaintance on the force, and...whatever. No need to get into the details. The point is, I've got it."

"And she's where?"

"Brooklyn. Her name's Amelia Warner. She's the captain of her cheerleading squad. Very pretty. She's eighteen. She got held back her senior year. Apparently, she failed almost all of her classes last year."

"How do you know that?"

"I got her transcripts too."

"And she's a student where?"

"A school called Columbus, a private school in Williamsburg."

"Give me everything you've got on her. Do you think she'll talk to me if I call her?"

Perez hesitated a moment. "In cases like this, victims often don't want to open up to a complete stranger. I wouldn't up and call her out of the blue. I don't think it will get you anywhere. If it really matters to you what this Jules did, I'd try to make the trip to see her."

Shit! How am I going to just take off for New York right now? Once I'd jotted down all of Amelia's contact information, I slipped my phone into my back pocket and thought it through. I hadn't missed a single day of work since I'd started at the school; I could call in sick for once.

On my break period, I went to the teachers' lounge and bought myself a ticket to New York that very night. I didn't know what I'd say to my brother and mother to keep them from bombarding me with questions, but I figured I could come up with something. Maybe I wouldn't even mention the trip—I'd just say I was hanging out with Maggie.

Speaking of whom...

She walked in with a huge smile on her face just as I was reviewing my travel details. Then she saw me. And it disappeared. "I didn't know you were in here," she said, shutting the door behind her. In fact, I was the only one in there.

"Is that weird or something?" I asked, trying to soften the mood.

"What's weird is me seeing you at all," she said, throwing her bag on the table and pouring herself a coffee.

"You know how it goes," I said, but she was right. We'd been seeing each other often, with me staying over at her house, and then, all of a sudden, I stopped calling her. "So what's up?" I asked, unsure how to start a conversation.

She turned around and glared at me with her bright-blue eyes.

"What's up? Thiago, you stopped calling me! No messages; you totally ghosted me!"

"Did I?"

"And now you have the balls to act surprised?! I swear, you're unbearable."

"Hey! Calm down, all right?" I stood up and walked over to her. "I'm sorry if I've been distant. I've had a lot of things going on at home."

"I don't care, Thiago," she said, stirring her coffee. "You're one of those guys who thinks you can just apologize to a girl and have her eating out of the palm of your hand no matter how many times you've fucked up. Well, sorry, but that's not me."

I looked into Maggie's eyes, and I couldn't help but compare them to Kam's. Maggie had spectacular blue eyes, but they couldn't hold a candle to Kam's big brown eyes and long lashes. It wasn't about the color, dark or light, it was about what they transmitted when they looked at me. Kam had an endless well of mixed feelings swirling around her deep irises, never quite sure what to do next. When she and I looked at each other, something happened. Something special. Didn't she know that? Maggie was just a pair of pretty blue eyes. She might have been special, but I knew she wasn't right for me. There was an attraction there, but it was just physical.

"I warned you I wasn't an easy guy to get along with," I told her, though I knew that was no excuse. She was a good woman; she didn't deserve to be treated like trash.

"You did warn me," she agreed, "and that's why I'm going to start following your advice. We're done. I don't know what it is we have, or had, rather, but I don't need any problems at work, and I sure as hell don't want to be with someone who couldn't make a commitment if his life depended on it."

She was being a little overdramatic, and I had to choke back a laugh.

"Don't you laugh at me, Di Bianco!"

I raised my hands and snickered as she punched me in the arm. She was smiling. "Sorry, Maggs, I'm sorry, OK! We can still be friends, though, can't we?"

"Me, friends with you?" She turned her back to me, heading for the door.

"You're gonna have to see me every morning of every day in this miserable teachers' lounge. We might as well get along, right?"

"You're insufferable," she said over her shoulder.

"But you still like me."

She looked back, and the faintest smile appeared on her red lips.

When lunchtime came, I looked around for Kam despite myself. It was a habit at this point. She was sitting in the cafeteria with my brother and a couple of friends, looking nervous and forlorn.

Why the long face, sweetheart? You got what you wanted—or didn't you?

My instincts told me to get up, walk over, and hug her until a smile appeared on her pretty face. Then my eyes panned over and met my brother's. His expression wasn't very welcoming. I guess mine wasn't either. It was inevitable. There was going to be a confrontation between us sooner or later. And the scary thing was, I didn't even care.

Could the love of a woman mean more than the love of a brother? *No*, I told myself, *no*, but it could sure as hell mess things up. I wanted the best for Taylor, but he had the thing I most desired, and I was someone who played to win, whoever my opponent was.

You can't control your feelings, and my feelings for Kam were here to stay, no matter what went down with Taylor. Did I feel guilty? Sure. But I wasn't so sure I could ignore what was going on inside of me, feeling so destroyed day after day.

The afternoon went by quickly, or as quickly as it could when you were teaching PE to kids aged six to twelve, not to mention training older ones. I liked my job, though, and it started to dawn on me that I'd feel sad when they hired someone permanent.

I waited in the parking lot to drive Kam and my brother home. It was hard enough seeing them together every day, watching them flirt and pretend I wasn't there. I couldn't stop myself from looking at her in the rearview mirror, but the worst part was when she looked back at me with those eyes of hers. Her gaze often seemed to be screaming for me to help her—rescue her, hug and kiss her, give her the world. Other times she seemed angry and serious. When our eyes met, it wasn't long before she looked away, staring steadily out the window until our houses came into view.

I pulled into her driveway—I usually parked in mine—and Kam and Taylor got out. He always walked her to her door and said goodbye to her with a kiss on the lips.

I couldn't watch that again.

Not today, anyway.

"Valet service," I said, trying to ease the tension. Kam and my brother got out of the car. I heard him tell her he loved her and that they would talk later. She said she'd call him and then went inside. When Taylor got back in the car, he had a confused look on his face. "What the hell's up with you?" I asked him as I put the car in reverse and pulled back out into the street.

"What's up with me? What the hell's up with you, Thiago? This has gone too far."

I parked, cut the engine, and removed the key.

"What's gone too far?" I asked.

"You looking at Kami like she's your girlfriend and not mine."

I held my breath a moment, trying to relax before firing back: "What the fuck are you talking about, Taylor?" I saw the fight coming, but I wanted to avoid it because I wasn't sure our relationship would make it through it intact.

"What the fuck am I talking about? Do you think I'm blind?"

I got out, and he did the same. He came around to me, and I had to remind myself that he was my brother and I shouldn't start a fight, least of all over a girl.

"There's nothing between Kam and me," I said, and I could taste the hypocrisy on my tongue.

"You son of a bitch. How dare you lie straight to my face. She told me, Thiago! The difference is you can't stop looking at her like you want to fuck her."

"Well, maybe I do."

Why did I say that?

Because I was a jerk.

Because I was immature.

Because I thought I was tough when I was really a fool.

Because I wanted her for myself, but she wasn't mine, and I could feel that killing me day in, day out.

Taylor tried to shove me, but I knocked him away. He hit the car, and the alarm went off.

"Taylor, you don't want to take me on, and you know it," I said. I didn't wait for him to respond. I hurried upstairs and packed my bag for New York.

I sent Mom a message telling her I wouldn't be home that night, strapped on my backpack and hopped on my motorcycle. I'd finally finished repairing it the week before, but I hadn't wanted to use it because of the snow and cold. My leather jacket didn't do much to keep me warm, and by the time I left the bike in the parking garage at the airport, I was shivering.

I didn't have to check a bag, so I had a lot of time to wait. Finally, they called for boarding, and I got on and found my seat. I'd booked a cheap room in Brooklyn so I could reach the girl's school on the subway without having to walk a thousand miles to get to Williamsburg. I got to my hotel around midnight. I had Amelia Warner's number in my phone. I wanted to call her—I was desperate to find out as soon as possible what the hell was going on—but I knew it was best to wait until the next day. I did send a message to one important person, though.

For once in your life, I'm begging you, listen to me and don't trust Julian. I promise I'll explain soon enough.

I got no response.

I had a bad feeling when I went to bed. I couldn't stop thinking to myself that whatever I discovered the next day, it was bound to change everything.

The alarm sounded early. I still didn't know how exactly I was going to convince this girl to talk to me, but I did know I'd have to get out of bed first.

The hotel was a dump, and I had tossed and turned all night; the mattress was nothing more than a jumble of springs sticking out in every direction. I got dressed and hurried out before dawn to soak up that amazing, chaotic city.

My plan was to try to intercept Amelia on her way out of school. According to what I could find on the internet, classes ended at three. Since I had time to kill, I took the subway to Manhattan, and in half an hour I was strolling around Central Park. The cold had let up a bit, and at twelve, I took a seat on a bench and started reading a half-finished book. As I did, I heard a soft voice, and I looked up to see an attractive woman talking to her son, who must have been around four or five years old.

I said son, but who knew—maybe he was her little brother? Because she was pretty young—a few years older than me at most.

"Noah, come on!" came a man's voice further up the path. "It was supposed to be funny."

"Don't listen to him, Andy, we're staying right here," she said to the little boy. "To hell with Daddy, right?"

"Yeah, to hell with Daddy."

Noah seemed to regret those words as soon as they came back at her from the little boy's mouth. Her cheeks turned red, and she said, "Good lord, son, you don't have to repeat everything that comes out of Mama's mouth."

"Daddy, Mama's mad at you!" the boy yelled. I caught a glimpse of his face under his wool hat. He had striking sky-blue eyes.

"No kidding. Who'd have ever guessed?" the father said. By now he had walked back to where they were standing. They looked like a typical rich couple without a care in the world. She was pretty and young and looked sweet. He was the stereotype of a Wall Street stockbroker in his impeccable suit and polished shoes. He took hold of the little boy's hand.

I couldn't help but roll my eyes. Couldn't at least one of them have been ugly or old?

"Freckles, it was a joke, OK?"

"There was nothing funny about it!" she said, showing some gall under that sweetness.

"But everyone was laughing," the guy said, covering the kid's ears so he wouldn't hear them arguing.

"Yeah, laughing at me! You find that amusing, do you now?"

"They were laughing *with* you, babe."

"Don't you dare call me *babe* right now!" she said, pointing a finger at him. "I'm going back to the apartment right now to call all the guests and cancel that goddamned fucking party, you'd better believe it!"

"But why? Why do you care?"

"Because you didn't even bother to fucking ask me, Nicolas! What would you think if I decided to open an account in your name with a million dollars in it, huh?"

Dumbstruck, I was dying to know what he'd say. But just then the strapping man seemed to notice I was staring at them. He took his eyes off his wife just long enough to give me a nasty look before turning back to her.

"Could you keep your voice down, please? Are you trying to get robbed?"

I stuck my nose back in my book, pretending like I couldn't hear a thing...

"If somebody comes along and steals that indulgent sum of money from the account you set up in my name, all the better!"

"Oh, God," he said, picking his son up in his arms and pulling the woman toward him. "That money is yours, whether you like it or not, my love. Don't waste your time arguing with me about it." Just when she was about to fire something back, he planted a kiss on her lips.

I watched them out of the corner of my eye. You didn't have to be a genius to see there was something real there. That's how it could be with Kam and me. Maybe I'd never be able to open her an account with a million dollars in it, but I knew I could get under her skin like that, and a thousand other ways too.

"Don't think one kiss is enough to get you out of the doghouse, mister," the woman said.

"Yeah, mister," the kid said. He was clearly enjoying all this.

"I've got to go see Cortez now. But I promise tonight I'll make it up to you—you'll forgive me for giving you a million dollars."

Noah crossed her arms, and a smile appeared on her gorgeous lips. "You're unbelievable."

"You love me, though, don't you?" the guy said. I didn't get to hear her response because he'd started kissing her again. I couldn't take it anymore, so I got up and left. It wasn't long before I'd need to catch a train back to Brooklyn, so I decided to grab a bite at a sandwich joint and think over what I was going to say to the girl before she literally sent me packing.

I got to Williamsburg twenty minutes before school let out, and I leaned against the building across the street, watching people come and go. When the bell rang and school ended, I had to look at the photo of Amelia a few times to make sure I'd recognize her as she walked out.

Eventually a thin girl with light-brown hair came out wearing the school uniform. She was chatting and laughing with a group of friends. I knew it was going to be weird if some random man stopped them to talk, so I tried to be as polite as possible, walking up to them in the middle of the street. Amelia had a girl on either side of her, all wearing the same pleated green and navy-blue skirt with matching shirt and jacket.

"Excuse me," I said to them. "I'm sorry to interrupt." I tried to smile in a friendly way.

"Can we help you?" Amelia asked as the three of them looked back and forth at each other. *Fuck. I didn't expect such a nice response and such a quick one.*

One of her friends whispered something to the other one, and they both blushed. Did they think I was cute or something? Well, that could actually work in my favor.

"Yeah, I was actually looking for you," I said, pointing at Amelia. She was a typical pretty girl: long straight hair, full lips, and striking green eyes. She was gorgeous...and she knew it. Actually, she reminded me of Kam.

"Me?" she asked, seeming flattered.

"Yeah. It's about something... Look, I know this is weird, but could I possibly buy you a coffee?"

She hesitated, and one of her friends nudged her with her elbow, trying to be sly about it. I saw it, but I pretended I hadn't.

"I don't even know you," she said. At least now I knew she wasn't dumb enough to go off with some stranger.

"Just a coffee. At that Starbucks right over there. I'll buy," I added using my most seductive smile.

Amelia thought it over a few seconds and then agreed. "Fine," she said, and turned to her friends. "I'll see you later. If I don't text you in the next two hours, call the police." She was joking, I knew, but that still put me on edge.

When her friends left, turning back repeatedly to stare at us, I gestured for Amelia to follow me. Inside, she ordered a mocha, and I told her to have a seat. I ordered the same, and five minutes later I was sitting across from her, each of us with our own paper cup.

"So, for starters, my name's Thiago Di Bianco. Sorry I didn't mention that before. I flew up from Carsville to talk to you. I need to know anything you can tell me about Jules Murphy. Anything."

Amelia was just about to take a sip, but she froze. Panic appeared in her green eyes. And I knew I'd been right to make the trip.

Julian Murphy was dangerous.

And I was about to find out why.

CHAPTER TWENTY-ONE

Thiago

She turned pale, and her hand started to tremble ever so slightly.

"Why are you here? Did he send you? I did everything he asked."

I paid close attention to those words. To the way she talked to me, and how she immediately got so defensive. But that's not all, it's how scared she was. The fear behind her eyes told me everything I needed to know. She couldn't hide it. Something bad had happened. And I wasn't going to like what I heard.

"Amelia, it's OK...relax." I tried to sound calm. "I'm not here to hurt you. I promise. I'm here to find out about Jules because something tells me he's dangerous, and I'm worried he might be about to hurt someone else."

Amelia looked around and stood up.

"Sorry, you've got the wrong person," she said. I put my hand on her wrist to stop her and tried to stay calm. I didn't want to scare her.

"Please don't go," I asked, "I'm scared that a friend is in danger because of him, and I need to know what's going on before I make the wrong decision."

She looked at me doubtfully.

"Please," I repeated. "All I need to know is what he did and why you asked for a restraining order against him."

Surprised now, Amelia sat back down. Not because she wanted to talk to me, it seemed, but because she was worried her legs wouldn't hold her up much longer.

"How do you know about that?" she asked.

"Does it matter? Look: Jules is a new student at the school where I work as a coach. I had a feeling I'd seen him before and—don't let this weird you out—I had. We met in jail one day when I was a little younger, we both got arrested, and we were assigned the same holding cell. Don't be scared. I got in a fight, nothing serious. It was a dumb mistake. But I remember meeting him there and that he used to go by a different name. At the school where I work, everyone calls him Julian Murphy."

"Jules is crazy," she said. "That's all you need to know."

"What did he do to you, Amelia?"

She looked out the window, picked up her cup, and took a sip.

"He was a sweetheart at first, OK?" She spoke without looking at me. "I'm a good student, but I've always struggled with math. It's been that way since I was a kid, and someone told me Jules was tutoring people for free. So I got in touch with him and started lessons. At first, he gave them in the library, but eventually he was like, *Oh, you should come to my house or let me come to yours*, and that made sense because it was more relaxed and we could meet whenever we wanted. We got along, and he's good-looking too. I was the head cheerleader then, and he was kind of a nerd, so...you get it, I wasn't used to being seen with people like him. When we first started going out, we kept it a secret. I know that was wrong, I know now, but it's high school. I didn't want people to know I was with some math geek. Especially because Liam... Liam's the captain of the rugby team and he ended up being homecoming king that year; he was into me, and I think people sort of hoped we'd end up being a thing. I know Liam did."

All these details seemed irrelevant, except for the fact that I might as well have been listening to Kam describing herself. Amelia seemed a little more superficial, but they had more similarities than differences.

"Go on," I encouraged her.

"We hadn't been together for long before he turned super demanding. He kept asking for more and more. I could have been nicer to him, I admit that, but it's just that our lives were so different. He used to say all the people at school were assholes, that I was better than them, that I shouldn't even bother hanging out with them. He never wanted to go anywhere; he just wanted to hang out in his room. And soon he... I don't know how to explain it, but he managed to drive me away from all my friends. He'd be there waiting for me outside the door of all my classes; he'd pick me up and take me home from school. People found out about us, of course, and some people thought it was weird."

Who cared what other people thought? I wanted to ask her that, but I held back. I was starting to get what kind of girl Amelia Warner was. Although they had some similarities, this girl couldn't compare to Kam. Then, Amelia started getting nervous, and tears streamed from her eyes.

"I wanted to break up with him. Once we slept together, everything got worse. He turned obsessive. He wouldn't leave me alone for a second, and he started threatening to hurt my friends. He said they deserved whatever they got because if I was so superficial and empty, it was because of them. And he always knew everything! I don't know how, but he kept track of who I talked to, who I saw..." She glanced at me a moment and her cheeks flushed an even darker crimson. "Then, the last time we slept together...

he took it too far. He liked to experiment, and at first, I was OK with trying new things. He had promised if I didn't like something, I could just say our safe word and he'd stop. But he didn't... He tied me up, hands and feet, and he brought out a video camera..."

I tensed up when I heard that. "He recorded you?"

Amelia nodded.

"He recorded all of it." She wiped a tear from her face with the back of her hand. "He told me he was going to post it online, and that's when I called the cops. People figured out he was a psycho. You can't imagine the stuff he was into. He knew everything about everyone, and I found out it wasn't just me he was blackmailing. It was my friends too, even people who just kind of knew me."

"So why didn't you end up pressing charges?"

"Because he threatened to put the video online," she said simply. "The police couldn't do anything about something they weren't even sure existed. They arrested him because I told them what he'd done to me, but I withdrew the charges when I found out that, if he wanted, that video would be all over the internet, haunting me for the rest of my life."

That piece of shit.

It was him.

My instincts had been right the whole time.

"By then he had a bad rep at school, and I guess he decided to leave before they kicked him out. My friends did beat the shit out of him, though." Her look was defiant as she told me this, almost as if she were daring me to challenge her. "He was an outcast then, and it seems like he's still an outcast now."

I needed to tell Kam and my brother. I needed to let the school know. Julian was the one who had pushed everyone away from Kam. That was his MO. He was the one who had uploaded the video. How had he gotten it, though? Maybe he and Danny were in cahoots? Who knows.

"Thanks, Amelia. What you've just told me..." I was too furious to finish the sentence. I was far from home, and all I wanted was to disappear right then, to be near Kam so I could protect her and beat that bastard to a pulp if he even tried to get close to her.

"He takes advantage of your misfortunes. That's how he gets to you. He's a typical psychopath," she concluded.

"Do you think," I asked, "that he could be violent, apart from blackmail and manipulation?"

Amelia looked me square in the eye. "I think Jules is capable of anything if he thinks it will get him what he wants. He's obsessed with popularity and with this idea that the way girls are raised makes them stupid and superficial. He used to say that a lot, that I was better than those stupid bitches at school and I needed to act like it..."

I stood. I needed to go. Now. Amelia grabbed my hand and stopped me.

"If you tell Jules what I told you, he'll come for me." Her eyes filled with tears. "He will. He swore it. And he still has the video. Please, help your friend, but leave me out of this. I'm begging you."

"Don't worry," I said, hoping to calm her down. "I promise I won't bother you again."

Amelia didn't seem convinced, but I didn't stay long enough to tell her what I thought: that she could put him out of her mind because I wouldn't stop until he was behind bars.

I went straight back to the hotel, grabbed my things, and caught a cab. Once I was at the airport, I texted my brother:

Make sure Kam stays away from Julian. He's dangerous. I'll tell you more later. For now, just keep him away from her.

The plane took off on time, but it seemed like the longest hour and a half of my life. When we landed, I looked at my phone to see if Taylor had answered and, sure enough, there were two messages from my brother.

What are you talking about?

Where are you?

Once I got back to my bike in the parking lot, I sent him another message:

I'm on my way home. Don't go to bed.

It took me a while to get there—the airport was a ways from town—and by the time I made it, all the lights were off at my place and at Kam's. I wasn't surprised since it was pretty late, but when I walked upstairs and saw the light under my brother's door, I knew he'd done as I'd asked. I knocked before opening. When he told me to come in, I saw he wasn't alone. Kam was there, wearing one of my brother's shirts. My brother was sitting in his swivel chair, and he spun around to look at me. I wanted to hug Kam and tell her everything would be OK, but I stopped myself as my brother asked, "What's up, Thiago? What's the deal with Julian?"

I shut the door behind me. "First off, his name isn't Julian, it's Jules." I told them everything I'd found out, the entire story from the beginning, starting with when I saw him in the cell and how it reminded me of meeting him before, and finishing with my quick trip to New York to hear Amelia Warner's story. They listened closely, struggling to believe it. Kam was white as a sheet when I was done.

"I'm gonna kill him," Taylor said, getting to his feet. I held him back.

"We need to think about how to deal with the situation now. We still don't have any proof."

"Taylor, let me see the video," Kam said, interrupting us.

"What?"

"You've got it, right? You told me that someone sent it to you in a text, right? Not via Instagram," she said.

"OK, but why?"

"Taylor, just show it to me."

Tay scrolled around in his phone, then passed it to Kam, who took it in her trembling hands. I didn't understand what was happening. What she was looking for, what she thought she'd find in it.

"Jesus," Kam said, covering her mouth.

"What?" I asked.

"It wasn't Danny," she said. "Danny's not the one who recorded me. It was Julian," she said, dropping the phone suddenly, as if it were burning her hands.

"What?" my brother said.

"It was the day of the game against Falls Church. Oh my God…" She started crying. "He drugged me. He drugged me that night. That's why I couldn't remember falling asleep. That was why I didn't get up on time and was late to practice!"

My face flushed with rage.

"Are you sure?" I asked, trying to control the anger and the sense of powerlessness coming over me.

"Look at the video," she said, her voice cracking. "See the wall? It's the same color as the walls at the motel. I didn't realize it until you told me all this stuff. How didn't I realize…? I erased the video immediately. I was so ashamed…"

"Why would Julian do something like this?" my brother asked.

"Because he's in love with her," I said, imagining myself beating him to a pulp.

"Julian's gay," Taylor objected, looking confused.

"He's not in love with me," Kami said. "We're supposed to be friends." She stood up, as if moving around could somehow help prove that this nightmare wasn't actually real.

"Julian's no gayer than you or me, Taylor," I said, walking over to my brother's desk and opening his laptop. I sat back on the bed and searched for the page Perez had sent me. "Look what Perez found," I said, showing it to them.

Kam examined it and shook her head. "I can't believe it," she said, sitting back down on the bed beside me. "Look! There's a comment from a couple days ago that says *'THEY'LL ALL BURN IN HELL'* and it's from @omv_ovamat; that's the same username that was leaving comments on my Instagram."

"What the hell does @omv_ovamat mean?" I asked, disgusted.

"No idea," Kam replied. "I can't believe it. I can't believe the way he lied to me, deceived me…"

"At least we finally know who was behind it all," Taylor said, but it didn't seem to help much.

"Listen," she said, standing, "I need to be alone, I need… I need to go." I could see the panic, the sorrow flooding her brown eyes. I stood too. But why? What was I going to do? Hug her? Tell her everything was OK? I couldn't. I couldn't because she wasn't my girlfriend, she was my brother's girlfriend.

"I'll walk you home," Taylor said, standing.

I looked at the computer again and then closed it.

In the doorway, Kam turned back. "Thanks, Thiago. For everything. For going to New York, for looking into this even though it wasn't your problem. Honestly, thank you."

I nodded. *I did it because I love you*, I wanted to tell her, but one look at my brother was all I needed to tell me how angry he was that I had figured things out about Julian instead of him. They walked out, and I went to my room.

What am I going to do about you, Jules? I asked myself. *Take care of you for good and ruin my life in the process?*

I didn't sleep a wink that night.

Worst of all, there would be many sleepless nights to follow. There are times when I go back to that moment and I tell myself I should have followed my instincts, because getting him out of the way would have been the best choice.

Because if I had, it would have saved a lot of lives.

CHAPTER TWENTY-TWO

Kami

I COULDN'T SLEEP ALL NIGHT.

Julian was Momo.

Julian was the bad guy.

Julian was the one who'd made that video and uploaded it to the internet.

Julian had pushed my friends away.

Why?

Why?

Why?

I couldn't stop asking myself. I couldn't understand why he had lied. Tricked me. Used me. Manipulated me.

Why did people like that exist?

But the worst was that I couldn't get my head around how deep Julian's manipulation had gone. He was a psychopath. He was the worst kind of psychopath, and at the time I still didn't realize just how dangerous he was.

I thought of Kate. She was living under the same roof as someone completely deranged. The same guy who had written all those horrible messages under the pseudonym @omv_ovamat.

I thought of my brother... That bastard had been tormenting my poor little brother. He'd scared Cam enough to make him
sneak into my room and steal my photos. He'd probably asked
him to do other things: tell him where I went, who I was with...

Jesus!

What would I do when I saw him?

What would I do when he popped up with that fake smile
stretching from ear to ear and I had to tell him that I knew everything? That I knew who he was, what his real name was. What he
was doing, how he had lied to me.

I was scared. When things like this happen, you never know
what it could lead you or others to do. I was scared, and I felt
rejected. Rejected by my friends. I had tried to be real, to be
sincere, and where had it gotten me? All my ideals and beliefs
seemed to be collapsing in around me just because one psychotic
weirdo had decided to manipulate me and everyone close to me.

I thought of Thiago. Of everything he had done for me,
everything he'd done to get to the bottom of what was going
on. I thought of how he looked at me, how he tried to protect
me, and those messages he'd written warning me about Julian. I
thought of how I'd ignored him because I'd thought he was just
jealous.

Things were bad, and I was even more scared of how they
might turn out.

I thought of Danny. He was a dickhead, but he didn't deserve
what had happened to him. He'd been beaten up, shunned, called
a rapist. That was my fault. I had never doubted he was behind all
this; he was the only person who made sense.

Now I understood the importance of evidence.

You're innocent until proven guilty, right? And yet the entire
school, including me, had judged him for a crime he didn't commit.

I couldn't fix it.

But I needed to try.

I needed to say I was sorry.

I needed to let him know that he, too, was a victim of Julian.

Julian had piled on with everyone else, landing Danny in the hospital, supposedly to defend me!

How could a person be so horrible?

I called Danny and waited for him to pick up. It was around seven in the morning. Soon I'd be seeing everyone at school. I was scared of that, and I was scared of what Danny would say, but he needed to know what Julian had done.

"Yeah," he said groggily.

"Danny, it's me." I knew I was probably the last person in the world he'd want to hear from.

"What do you want?" he asked bitterly.

"There's something you should know..."

––––––––

Thiago and Taylor drove me to school that day.

"As soon as we get there, I'm going to the principal," Thiago said. "I'll tell him everything I know. If we're lucky, they'll expel him on the spot. After that, you can go straight to the police, Kam. That fucker's going to pay for what he's done, for all his manipulation and lies."

I was nervous. I didn't want to see Julian; how could I talk to someone so two-faced?

"Don't say anything to anyone else yet," Thiago went on. "Things are already bad enough, and..."

Shit.

"Thiago, Danny knows," I interrupted him. Taylor and Thiago looked at me in the rearview mirror.

"You told Danny?" Thiago shouted.

"I needed to apologize. People were calling him a rapist!"

"Dammit, Kamila! Danny Walker's not going to wait for this to be solved peacefully!"

Thiago was right, we realized that as soon as we pulled into the lot. Everything seemed to happen in slow motion. Danny was leaning on his SUV. Waiting. His friends were with him. So they knew too, just as we did. Word got around fast in Carsville. I wouldn't have been surprised if the entire school knew. We didn't even have time to get out of the car.

Julian was nearing the entrance when Danny and his friends surrounded him.

"Shit," Thiago said.

"Don't get involved," his brother told him.

We were frozen in place. Were we wrong to stay back? Maybe. Probably. But sometimes people are more animal than human... and this was one of those times.

"So, you like lying to people, manipulating people?" Danny said. "You think it was funny to turn the whole school against me?" Everyone's eyes were on him.

Julian looked around, not understanding what was happening.

"Did it make you feel like a man to punch and kick me in this parking lot, to break my arm?" Danny motioned to his friends, and they grabbed Julian by the arms so he couldn't fight back.

"Let me go! What the fuck are you talking about? Why are you all defending him? He's a fucking rapist!"

Danny's fist struck Julian's face, and blood splattered the ground. A crowd closed in on them, and we had to get out of the car and move closer to see what was happening.

Was I happy he was getting what he deserved?

Yes.

Did that make me a bad person?

Maybe.

But he had deceived me in every possible way. Julian Murphy had violated my trust, sexually assaulted me, he'd made me a laughingstock, an outcast.

And he needed to pay.

People moved aside to let us through. When Julian saw me, his expression changed.

"Kam, tell them to leave me alone!" he shouted with fear in his eyes.

Julian, scared?

That was something new.

I didn't say a word.

I just stood there.

Watching.

And that made me as guilty as anyone for what happened and what was to come.

That's something I'll never forgive myself for.

"Julian Murphy lied to all of us! He's the one who spray-painted the lockers! He's the one who put that video of Kami on Instagram! He's the rapist!" Danny shouted.

"I didn't rape anyone!" Julian shouted, staring at me.

Again, Danny hit him in the face, using his good arm. "You liked that? Taking off Kami's clothes and recording her without her permission?"

I felt my hands and legs starting to shake. Taylor, whose arm had been around my shoulder, stepped forward, and his brother instinctively embraced me.

"I'm going to kill you, you son of a bitch," Taylor said, stepping closer to Julian.

Julian's head was down. The crowd seemed nervous. Thiago was as tense as a bowstring. Taylor punched Julian.

Danny cheered. "Who else wants to give this liar and manipulator what he deserves?"

Everyone was shouting and cursing.

"You know what I'm going to do?" Danny said. "Exactly what you did to Kami, you piece of shit."

"I need to get out of here," I told Thiago, but he just hugged me tighter, he didn't move.

"Take off his clothes," Danny told his friends.

Taylor didn't participate. He just stood there watching as Danny's friends did what he said, laughing the whole time.

Julian wriggled and screamed, "Leave me alone!"

"Come on, take out your phones! Record him! Put it all over the internet! After all, that's what you did, isn't it, Julian?"

Danny kicked Julian in the stomach, and he doubled over in pain. Taylor seemed to be supervising the whole thing. I wanted to get out of there; I didn't want to be a part of this. Even if he deserved it, what they were doing wasn't right. I believed in justice, and abiding by the law...

"Stop it!" Julian cried, but it was pointless. People were laughing. They stripped him naked as he crouched down, scared of getting hit again. Everyone snapped photos and took videos of him on their phones.

It wasn't right.

It wasn't right at all.

I was asking myself what would happen next when the principal and a bunch of teachers showed up. The last thing I saw before Thiago spun me around and whisked me away was Danny spitting in Julian's face.

People dispersed in all directions. I noticed Kate was there, frozen, unable to believe what was happening.

"Come on, get in the car!" Thiago said, jumping into the driver's seat.

"What about Taylor?" I asked as he started the engine. I couldn't see him through the throng of students.

"Don't worry about him. He probably ran off with the rest of them." Thiago turned onto a quiet street. "We're going to wait here for a little bit. I can't have anyone thinking I was involved," he said, resting his forehead on the steering wheel with a long sigh.

"Are you afraid of getting in trouble with the principal?" I asked as my heartbeat slowed to normal.

"I'm more afraid of losing control and doing something I'd regret if I see that piece of shit again."

He eventually lifted his head and looked over, and in the silence, I felt my fear vanish.

"You didn't deserve this, Kam," he said, stroking my cheek.

I closed my eyes. He went on: "And I won't stop until I know you're safe at that damn school."

"Thiago, you don't have to keep worrying about me. You've done more than enough."

"Nothing's too much when it comes to you, Kam."

I blinked and tried to keep from crying.

"I love you," Thiago said. And for a moment, I was speechless.

"I have so many things I want to tell you," I managed to say as he carefully wiped away my tears.

"Tell me in secret, and I promise whatever you say will stay with me forever."

I looked into his beautiful green eyes, and I had to say it.

I couldn't keep holding it in forever.

"I love you too, Thiago. I always have."

EPILOGUE

Julian

THEY HAD HUMILIATED ME.

They had treated me like an animal.

I seethed as I looked at the images that had been plastered all over social media. I raged as I saw my naked body being joked about, turned into memes, cut and pasted into degrading scenarios. And I made a list of each and every person who had liked, commented on, or shared it.

This wasn't the end.

I felt the adrenaline coursing through my veins, giving me strength.

I sat at my computer and opened my special folder. The one with the videos, the emails, the photos, the text messages. I had something on everyone. I knew their secrets, and I was going to use them.

But that wasn't enough. That wouldn't placate my rage. There was only one person who could've made me feel better.

I'd sent her a message asking for forgiveness, but I hadn't gotten a response.

I kept checking my phone over and over, and finally it came

through. My heart was pounding, and I felt dizzy as I saw her name on the screen.

You're the most despicable person I've ever met. Don't speak to me ever again. Don't even look at me. I hate you, Julian. You deserve all of it and more.

My heart rate steadied, and I forced myself to remain calm.

Kam wouldn't turn her back on me.

Kam was mine.

Everything I'd done was to make her mine, to help her understand she deserved better than all those morons we went to school with. She was a queen. She was gorgeous. She was elegant. She was the most beautiful girl I'd ever met.

I clenched my fists as I heard a knock at my door. I stood and opened it. There she was, my little lapdog. "Come on in, Kate," I said, standing aside. My sister walked in, staring at the floor, the way I'd taught her.

"What are you going to do, Jules?" she asked, paralyzed with fear.

I closed the door and sat down on my futon.

"What am I going to do about what?"

"People know it was you. Are you going to transfer to another school again?" She was so stupid; she thought I wouldn't be able to detect the hopeful tone in her voice.

"You honestly think I'm going to up and leave after what they've done to me? After how they've treated me?" I screamed.

Kate flinched and stepped back.

"I...I can't do it anymore."

"You can't do what anymore?" I stood and stepped toward her. "You'll do exactly what I tell you to do. You'll keep behaving exactly as you have up to now, understand me?"

Kate pursed her lips.

"Or did you forget what could happen if the videos of us came out? You do remember what you and I did together, don't you? And how much you liked it? How you kept begging me for more?" I said, knowing I had her under my thumb for life.

Kate started crying, and I made a sad face, mocking her.

Girls are all so predictable...

"Now get out of here. I'm not in the mood to deal with you today."

Kate walked out, and I climbed the ladder to my loft, where I had a bed and a small TV. Kate's mom and my dad never went up there, and that was where I could enjoy my little collection. All over the walls were photos I'd taken of Kam. Kam sleeping, Kam naked, Kam laughing, Kam with Thiago, Kam with Taylor, Kam with her brother, Kam with her father, Kam's eyes, Kam's shiny hair, Kam's legs, Kam's chest, Kam cheerleading, Kam buying groceries...

How it turned me on, following her everywhere and capturing her with my camera lens.

She was so beautiful...she was perfect.

Kam had to be mine. She had to give up everyone else and stay by my side. I'd make her a better person. All those jerkoffs at school were ruining her. She was too good for them. After all, look how easily they'd shut her out, with hardly any effort on my part.

They all had their dirty secrets, it had been easy enough to find them out. And when @omv_ovamat started threatening them, they'd all caved.

The only one who had put up any resistance at all was Ellie. But who touches themselves in front of their laptop with the camera uncovered? I got what I needed on her. In the end, she'd done what I'd said.

Getting her to hook up with Danny had been the final piece in the puzzle to make sure Kam felt even more lost, even more alone, even closer to me...

Everything had been going so well...

So how had I been discovered?

It had to be the Di Bianco brothers.

They were the ones who had fucked everything up.

I hated it when Taylor touched her, when Thiago looked at her... She was *mine*!

But it was no big deal. Soon enough, it would all be over.

At first, I'd thought this time might be different. I'd never gone to a school where everyone hadn't rejected me and called me a weirdo...But after what had happened that morning...

I opened the trunk at the foot of my bed. With what I had in there, I could finish off every one of them. And I'd still have plenty left over.

They had lit the wick.

And now, the dynamite was about to explode.

Acknowledgments

Each book is a new challenge. This is my pandemic book. I wrote it under a lot of pressure, with a lot of uncertainty and a lot of fear. Fear for my loved ones, fear of what might happen, fear of so many things that you all understand as well as I do because, maybe for the first time, we were all in the same boat.

I wrote this book as a form of escape for my readers, a window into the world as it used to be. It is filled with drama, danger, passion, and conflict, because that is who I am as a writer. But the true purpose of this book is to give you wings, to let you fly away and take a break from the strange reality we are all living in.

Everything's up in the air...except for one thing. My readers. No matter what, you're still there, reading voraciously. Thank you for getting to know my hidden side, a piece of me you can only understand if you submerge yourself in my many words and pages. Without you, all these stories would still be in my head.

Thank you to my editors at Penguin Random House in Spain, Rosa and Ada, for your patience and confidence in me and my abilities. Talking to you would cheer anyone up.

Thank you to Christa, Brittany, Holly, and the rest of the

amazing team at Sourcebooks for your support and for believing in my books.

And finally, thank you to my readers for staying with me. I will never get tired of writing stories as long as I know you are out there, ready to read them.

See you at #Tellmewithkisses.

About the Author

Mercedes Ron always dreamed of writing. She began by publishing her first stories on Wattpad, where more than 50 million readers were hooked on her books, and made the leap to bookstores in 2017 with Montena's imprint, launching the Culpables saga, a publishing phenomenon that has been translated into more than ten languages and has its own movie adaptation by Prime Video. Her success was followed by the sagas Enfrentados (*Ivory* and *Ebony*) and Dímelo (*Tell Me Softly, Tell Me in Secret, Tell Me with Kisses*), which consolidated the author as a benchmark in youth romantic literature with more than a million copies sold.